Broken Eye Books is an independent press, here to bring you the odd, strange, and offbeat side of speculative fiction. Our stories tend to blend genres, highlighting the weird and blurring its boundaries with horror, sci-fi, and fantasy.

Support weird. Support indie.

brokeneyebooks.com
twitter.com/brokeneyebooks
facebook.com/brokeneyebooks
instagram.com/brokeneyebooks
patreon.com/brokeneyebooks

THERE WAS A CROOKED MAN, BOOK 1

ALPHABET OF LIGHTNING
by EDWARD MORRIS

Published by
Broken Eye Books
www.brokeneyebooks.com

978-1-940372-64-8 (trade paperback)
978-1-940372-65-5 (hardcover)

Alphabet of Lightning

THERE WAS A CROOKED MAN, BOOK 1

Edward Morris

[PROLOGUE]

GANG OF FOUR ORIGINS

PART 1: MARA'SA

One Life, Furnished in Early Uchronian
2400 Earth CE

SOME TWINS ARE JOINED AT THE HIP THROUGHOUT LIFE IN QUAINT cliché. Mara and Samantha Walker had no use for *quaint* and less still for *cliché*. They weren't even identical: Sam was light-skinned with freckles, Mar as blue-black as onyx blasted by desert winds.

They shared the same liver, the same womb, the same legs. *Bon Dieu made us all*, Gran told the girls time and again. *Out of Mind, and to suffer.* There were never such devoted sisters in the history of Old Shang 2.

Gran was all for the Kybernoidia charity, the soldier-doctors and their Mutant Reintegration Programme. Anything they could get back from the Man. This was a bit of a contentious subject.

"Regrown bodies are too good to be true, just like everything else," their bio-mom said sometimes (when she wasn't too gacked-out on the hexomethamphetamine to form a sentence). "The bones leach. Seen it. You get like glass, like Mrs. Johnson did. Remember her? Three doors that way," she pointed.

Sam blurted, "The one who was"—both twins were beaming—"our size," Mar finished. "So . . . more fragile?"

Gran shook her head. "It's to do with minerals in the food, the water, the blood. Not enough. Some folks need more. Calcium. Old ladies like me too," she groaned, "who break their fool ankles bumping into that cussed stove. And inside"—she made a horrible face—"the organs, the new organs they grow for you that are supposed to be like yours, sometimes they . . . aren't. And the body rejects those parts. Or those parts just stop. Organ failure, the docs call it. Every kind I ever heard about, when I worked on that ward, before they let me go. Better off with the factory parts, my loves. I know it hurts . . ."

Mar and Sam remembered and jotted down and corroborated every single word. And the bellow came on a Saturday morning, a warm one, too warm to think or deal with two squalling twins presently cracking both Gran's eardrums in stereo: "You! Are—" "—NOT. CUTTING. US. IN—" "—half!!! No boy could split us up, so what makes you—" "—hey, wait a minute now—" "—not important, we—"

"Yeah, my mistake. Sorry." The girls' right hand waved a brochure from the National Institute of Biomedicine; their left fist shook in her face, but she pushed it away. "You two are willful. Why, you could both run and play and . . ."

"And die young," Mar sighed. "We run and play *now*, Gran. Mom says that—"

"Oh, your *mother* is just so full of—" Then she realized where she was and hushed, looking at the gray floor of the house she'd kept for nearly three generations just so these two little upstart crippled girls could—

She bit her lip, slamming on the brakes. She went into the front parlor and just sat for a while, looking around the well-kept little underground home she and that man of hers had built—forgive her sharp tongue—before Sam and Mar was even an *itch*. Her home, hewn from the rough rock by her man's two great big bloody black hands, so they could sit here and deny the rest of their life, down in the city. She could *pay*, she could . . .

"Gran," Mar said sadly, clearly reading her thoughts, "no matter how much you have in your mattress . . . hospitals are for . . . them. Not us. I'm—"

"—we're," Sam corrected, "going to school. We're going to be doctors. And we're not . . . cutting . . . a thing. I swear to Baby—"

"—Jesus and the Holy Ghost. We're going to work on the—"

"—rockets. Did we say somethin'?"

Gran's eyes swam with tears, but her voice never lost its rasp. "You both look so much like your mother. Like she did when she was a girl. And we used . . . we used to *do* things together, no matter what else was comin' down. We'd go to the park and read. I'd get her to read to me. Even when she was . . . oh . . ."

Her eyes squinched up like the numbers were coming through. "Four. Mina read to me when she was four. Words on a sign, it was. NON-GROUND LANE ONLY. A-ha-ha." All three of them shared the surprised laugh. "Of all the things you remember. Don't ever get old, kiddos. It makes ya goofy."

She shook her bony shoulders, tight bun of hair not moving an inch when her head did. "So you want to know mathematics like your Daddy did. Won't that just tie Mama's tail in a knot?"

Slowly, both heads went up and down. The light was long in the room. Hearts beat hard. And then Mara and Sam's great-grandmother Rita, Gran, grinned like an alligator with interesting dentures on top.

"Can you add and subtract?"

"Of course. We—"

"—do *fractions*, and we're just starting decimals, and—"

"Tutututut." Gran let her fluttering-flag hands take the air reproachfully, spotted as they were with the buckshot of years still standing. "You're in the army now. You will speak when spoken to."

"Is it a game?" Sam muttered, shrinking into her side of the dyad.

Gran simply winked, breath dancing over the equation from left field, from nowhere, "If $x = 10$ and $y = x - 6$, solve for y?"

The whispering campaign took no more than a second. Sam wrinkled up her adorable little nose. "Is it *four*?"

Gran knelt beside them and took both their hands. "I will teach you the greatest Vodou of all," she whispered matter-of-factly, "the kind you can take with you when you go"—she pinched either cheek—"to school. Either of you two rocket-surgeons remember where I put that old orange crate full of textbooks? The particular one that—"

"In the sub-cellar, right under the ladder," Sam said before Mar had time to pinch her. Mar did anyway.

"*Teacher's pet . . .*"

PENNSYLVANIA COLLECTION

[PACOLL]
Recovered Fragment,
Pennsylvania Collection; Letters
CD 18:A: Pre-1812 Americana, Rock Springs
Callaight County Library
Dr. Cricket Bennigan, orig. Redactor

10 November 1793

[here a line is struck out]

. . . in our present shattered situation, a full company muster cannot be expected from Callaight County. Our militia companies are entirely broken up, and whole townships laid to waste.

The communication betwixt our upper and lower districts is entirely broke, and our apprehensions of immediate danger are not lessened but greatly aggravated due to the distressed situation of the county.

Because of the strange incursions, many of the residents have already fled to the eastern counties of the state, so any victory may be pyrrhic or passing strange or somewhere betwixt.

Mr. President, my soldiers and I found that most, if not all, of the outlying houses were abandoned by the settlers. No Indians were encountered though. The army crossed over Locke Mountain near the southernmost end of the valley and arrived at the house of George Welsch, which unbeknownst to them had just been abandoned by the family.

UJ Smith made it known that Mr. Welsch had fortified his house completely but for arrow-slits betwixt the boards of each window-arch in order to defend it, if necessary, by force of arms. Reports from the ironmaster's home were wildly diverse. We found the house burnt to ashes but found no person killed at that place.

We decided to make camp upon the grounds, made and ate our night's repast, and then settled in for a sound and dreamless night's sleep, after which we awoke to find ourselves surrounded by debased white men painted and garb'd much in the manner of Indians.

These low men fasten'd combustible materials to their arrows, set them alight, and rain'd them upon our company. One must wonder why they felt the east face of the mountain to be a better place to massacre United States Army troops than the west face.

My men fired numerous rounds and arrows into the degenerates, which took a long time to lie down and decently die. Most of their number ran into the woods surrounding, like apes, and hid. This is a lot of ground, and we may be days in flushing them out.

The colonel and I found many of Rock Springs Garrison Commander Hammell's men tied to trees with numerous arrows pinning them there, the thongs cutting into their struggling flesh. The colonel noted that all the men had been scalped. He had the men cut down from the trees and buried at the spot.

Truly, such a scene of barbarism and desolation makes me want to find a canoe and go back out on the Monongahela River, past all those islands of trees that grow from living rock, and from there on to some point in Canada, north on the warpaths and deerpaths to the bright ice at the top of the world.

I care not who you are or where you have been, every man has a limit to how long he can look upon such things. I shall file my next memorandum upon this matter when I am a bit more Able, Mr. President, and I beg to remain,

Sergeant-at-Arms Donatien de Sade, Marquis

Chautaqua Garrisons, United States Army

In the Service of General Lafayette

GANG OF FOUR ORIGINS

PART 2: WHEELHORSE

2200 Earth CE

Eddie Donnellaigh was the sharpest salesman in Old Shang 2, and he'd tell yeh so too, to yer own face, lad. Why, not two days before the Terror marched right to the walls of the city proper (when his business was at its peak) and said a fine how d'y'do with their bedamned jelly mines they made from old tarpaulins and heat-fuse cord and the hoofs of Christ alone knew what . . .

In those lean, black-market years for the Boy Businessman, those hand-to-mouth days of dust and darkness where his childhood was as stolen as the changeling babe in the ancient Yeats poem, only then did Eddie learn the holiness of supply-side economics, supply and demand.

When he was eleven, just before, a man come to him at his lean-to in Cico Rabaud on the waterfront, the one he got to keep for several years before the Kybernoidia-pigs found where he spliced the power from the main grid, kicked down the walls, jack-rolled him for his poke, and told him to get lost.

That night while he slept on the loading dock of an abandoned cryo-warehouse, the man came. *He was just a man,* Eddie remembered. Didn't look like anyone, just some tosser in a gray houndstooth jacket sewn together from two vaguely similar jackets of vaguely similar pattern. Black tweed cap on his head. Sewer-mucker's boots. Could have been half a hundred yobs off the street.

Wasn't. "Yew, uhh, lookin' fur yur rent?" the man asked in an ugly, nasal Sticktown drawl. Eddie looked confused, already sitting up, shouldering his backpack. Already watchful. He hadn't been out of doors long, but he was starting to pick up the reflexes. (Eddie never took much time to learn anything.)

"I don't pay rent," Eddie answered. "No place to live. Not no more . . ." At that, the man knelt beside him, talking to him all slow and soothing—*Like I'm some sort of feeble-minded cripple in a bloody wheelchair,* Eddie thought with disgust.

"I've got a guest bedroom. It's warm. I . . . I don't get much company, and I could maybe make you some dinner, or—"

The man's eyes grew progressively glassier. Some weird part of Eddie saw the hand start to wander just before it did, and right when it got where it ought not, it found itself growing a little serrated pocketknife from the center thrice to the utmost pole.

Eddie bared his teeth . . . and dragged. His other hand forced the back of the man's head down, so he'd be confused. Like he had to do with his dad that time when he discovered how. Except now he had him a knife, and the tiniest bit more meat on his scrawny carcass.

The man howled like a banshee, falling to his knees. "I'm thirteen years old, you fuck," Eddie answered softly. The man was squirming. Eddie kicked out one foot, sent him flying flat, and was busily stripping his pockets before the man could even buck. When he did, Eddie head-butted him so hard in the face that he crumpled the rest of the way.

During the entire transaction, he never once had to get to his feet. Eddie was proud of that.

"Gotta spend money to make money," his da' always said (though, de facto, his da' was most concerned with spending money on the next bottle of whisky from the 'stillers down in Market Towne). Eddie found himself with so much venture capital, following that night, that his success in his field was terminal (until the Terror finally reset everything to a Zero Sum).

Even his dad said that the Lord helped those who helped themselves. True, the interpretation was a liberal one, but the sense of the aphorism seemed to point to him, with its many possible meanings, you could say . . .

But the next time Eddie remembered these things, he was delirious and far from acting on them immediately.

Everywhere in the tunnel now were the screams of the dead and the dying. Eddie hadn't prayed with the web-footed old village priest for nigh these five years, but he suddenly remembered the Rosary just fine . . .

It was all written, he thought, lying there on the old, cold stone floor, wheezing and bleeding out his life through the stump-mulch that had been his thighs, onto the rock that had made them so. *The Ancients all wrote it, those gods with the power to destroy a world. How, then, could their theories have been unsound?*

"Hail Mary, full of Grace, the Lord is with thee. Bless'd art thoo 'mong wummen 'n blest is d'fruit of dy woomb—"

Something almost but not quite too big to be a man loomed over him, reeking of testosterone and homemade gunpowder, and it was pushing away the boulder that cleaved him into a subtraction, a minus-sign, a *before* for which *something came after*, though he knew not what . . .

"MEDIC! I'M A MEDIC! DON'T TRY TO MOVE!" The howling voice was louder than the bomb that took his legs. Eddie looked way, way up at a mass of tattoos and hard scrap-hauler muscle. Anyone could see this soldier used to haul scrap by the radiation burns on his face and palms, but now he was . . .

"Jaisus," Eddie managed weakly as big sausage fingers he wouldn't have credited with the ability to tie a shoe started reaching in places and pinching off spurting arteries with the skill and grace of a chirurgeon.

Eddie looked up into the demon's painted face and saw yellow eyes, five days of beard, long knotted Plainfolk locks sticking out every which way. He saw a tentacled beast, a wolf, a saurian rearing down to eat his head at one bite, he . . .

"No, I ain't Jesus," the medic sighed. "Nick Coppersmith. Special Forces."

He whipped off his belt and looked at the buckle on Eddie's own. "You stay with me, son. You're the third live one I've found, and I got the other two topside. If you die on me, I will beat your ass. You know what morphine is? Good, 'cause you're gonna . . ."

The whole way up the tunnel, it felt like they were flying.

[. . . fragment is missing . . .]

A PEOPLE'S HISTORY OF CALLAIGHT COUNTY, PENNSYLVANIA
BY THE RIGHT REVEREND GEOFFREY DRADIN,
Lately of Belle Fonte, Pennsylvania,
Presently Waylaid by this Charm'd Countie
And Th' "Interesting Times" Within Her Borders.

Callaight County in the central region of the north woods of the Pennsylvania Colony, gateway to the Western Lands, was first settled by Scots-Irish trappers Nathan and William Powers between 1773 and 1775, out of lands obtained by treaty from the Monongahela in 1748.

Callaight County was originally calved off from the adjoining regions of Clinton, Potter, and Lycoming Counties, further calved most recently by mining concerns just due west in the Poe Mountain region, a somewhat larger area in geography with a greater concentration of coal to Callaight County's rich deposits of iron ore and limestone on the easternmost face of Locke Mountain where Ehrend Iron Smelting & Foundry turns on and on, the lynchpin of the wheel that is this county.

Rock Springs and the surrounding area sit on a bed of hard sandstone and shale, perhaps a seabed long ago. Before the first settlers arrived in the vicinity of what is now called Great Poison Swamp at Towne's Edge, this area was sacred ground to the Monongahela.

West of here, in the new Yuenger County, the few remaining Shawnee harvest the vast herds of deer that lock antlers around mating time. But the Shawnee do not venture down into this valley to hunt the bigger game unique to the region.

There are other hunters here I fain would speak of, for in speaking of them, I have lost my natural rights in the eyes of some members of the local gentry who would rather lure the unwary traveler into their towne and pick his pocket than stick out their thick red necks and rid the world entire of the abomination which may live in these mountains as a wolf lives among sheep—

The massacre of Nathan and William Powers, as well as Captain Ethan Plummer's Rangers, took place twenty miles west of the town Diamond, at the potter's field whence the new sanitorium was then being erected.

Ha! Ha! As if there were any health within these dank walls of beggar's mouldy travertine, any sanity to be had throughout the valley entire? O mighty, torrential river of mill-filth washing downstream in black coal-mine brimstone to gather poison like Acheron and swirl down the very blood-gutter of hell?

Marching forward along the trail, the Monongahela war party ambushed Capt. Plummer's scouting party and let out a loud war whoop. Apparently, the local militia were taken so completely aback that, not only did they not return fire, they threw down their arms and ran.

The rattle of musketry filled the air. Initially attacked as they attempted to gather their harvest near the Powers brothers' cabin and Seven Mile Trading Post, after surrendering to the Monongahela Chief Logan Black Rock's war party, fifteen colonial troops were driven quite out of their wits by ingesting of an unknown poison, most probably toadstools or deadly nightshade. Much of this has been lost to the forgetfulness of time.

Of seventy-five men in that company, seventy reinforcement troops sustained grievous injuries. Of the citizen population, many men and children perished. One white woman was taken by the war party. No one ever came to her rescue.

The only shot that was ever fired came from a gun surrendered by a ranger to Hayendeseh, son of Logan the sachem, who came a bit too close in the pursuit whilst his braves stripped the bodies and then left them scattered about (also a habit taught them by the rangers, like scalping).

The aforementioned Powers brothers, first to erect a cabin and trading post and to farm the land upon the spot, were subject to a gristlier fate of which decency forbids much discourse. However, even the base-court, common-kissing local historians in favor at the moment believe that this fate may have been perceived retribution for several rapings and ravagings of Monongahela womenfolk, girls, and one unnamed boy, still unsettled-for from earlier years.

The only part the court-favored historians will acknowledge reads thus, in part, from the local garrison commander to the Pennsylvania General Assembly:

"Sirs, I have to inform you that, on Sunday the third of this month, a party of rangers under Captain Plummer, fifteen in number, had an engagement with a party of Indians (said to be numerous) within three miles of Rock Springs where seventy-five of the border militia was station'd.

Commanded by Capt. Plummer, brought in seven wounded, eight kil'd and scalpt with their hands tyd and murdered in the most cruel manner.

Most remaining able-bodied militiamen, or those who choose to take arms, are wounded or have resign'd their commission. There is said to be others lost in the woods or missing.

This state of affairs has so alarmed the inhabitants that our whole settlement is upon the point of giving way. This countie at this time is in a deplorable situation. A number of families are flying away daily, ever since the late damage was done.

I can assure your excellency that if immediate assistance is not sent to this county, the whole of the frontier inhabitants will move in a few days. I am not convinc'd that any one settlement is able to make any stand against such numbers of the horde, be they the red-skinned savage or some other tribe we know not yet of. Both sources seem likely.

If your excellency should please to order us any assistance, less than a thousand men will be of but little relief to this county. Ammunition have we none. It is dreadful to think what the consequence of leaving such a number of helpless inhabitants may be to the cruelties of a savage race . . ."

The Common Weal, former colony and now state, of Pennsylvania, now has a provincial assembly and governor. From time to time, landed captains of industry petition the provincials to make a new county in their name. (William Penn set up the first ones last century.)

On September 11, 1787, lumber baron Joshua Douglas took out a patent from several of the same heirs of William Penn that made up the Supreme Executive Council of Pennsylvania. The large tract of mostly unsettled fertile bottom land along the Monongahela River, at the terminus of the Big Hot Spring and Nikolai Cave, is the oldest borough in the current borders of Callaight County, though new settlements seem to emerge almost daily.

There is one brewery, the Pierce; one distillery, the Frohsinn; and one freed

Negro slave, a mulatto gentleman, name of Brown, who speaks English better than most whites! Shylock's people are represented here too, enough Jews of German and Polish stock to have their own temple, a cunning stone structure called Temple Mogen David, in Old Towne very near to the American Hotel. That one is only one storey and also newly completed.

By 1792, this year, the year the Quakers say they will complete their hellish Bedlam-on-the-hill, there are forty houses yet in the village, salted along random avenues of activity in the valley.

There are about sixty blocks to the main part of Rock Springs village proper, centered on the hill at High and Wayne Streets: "Old Towne," served by the new canal and its towpath, the Lower Trail, along the Old Towne branch of the Monongahela at the southern extreme of Indian Valley. The limestone Lower Trail head leads to Alleghenia Village, thirteen miles to the east, and to Precious Crick, five miles west. This part of the Monongahela is an angler's paradise.

Even the black-robed Quaker bastards now have a fine new meetinghouse at Croyon Village, ten miles west through the woods along the foot of the Mountain of Sorrows (so named because the homo indomitus still secretly burns his dead commoners and buries his chieftains in the region, I may have noted).

Rock Springs has no clear centre as of yet. Even the streets of the ragtag-and-bobtail village, from the river southward, are laid out in two different grids based on whatever landowner claims to keep up said streets.

Not all of the alleys are nam'd, and there are warrens and multitudes of those with their ownership very often in dispute. The main street is High Street, which runs through the center of town.

A small cross street along the eastern side of the town common, or the Diamond, has already been named Washington Street. The ship of state turns tack, and quickly.

The place where the fine old houses and the public mall form a diamond is already a hub for holidays, parades, and other town fetes. I have seen the villagers caper and masque and throw hard candies into madding crowds at the one on All Hallows' E'en.

The barbarian Hibernian here decorticates the local gourds, carves the likeness of a skull in them, and uses it for a luminary! They say this is to honor their dead. I could think of several equally dedicated means that might involve less travail in their undertaking.

Hibernian and otherwise, the artisan class, in the form of many guilds, occupies a substantial part of the area. Leatherworkers, smitties, joiners, and potters nearly sit cheek by jowl in the Hinter-Lands. There are more dwelling around the riverfront harbor now, likewise more about the inn, even a good few dozen laborers, erecting new blocks of houses around the estates of various captains of industry, some with their own stores!

But every such neighborhood grows according to its own map, and after its own idiom. There will be complications, I fear, ones I surely shall not live to witness.

At present, said captains of industry are hard at work putting their wigs together to light a pyre under the projected Pennsylvania Canal's main line through town. The brothers Granson operate two stone quarries, Ehrend's solicitor runs the foundry into the ground, and round she goes.

The Monongahela River borders the town-ship, and Despond Crick flows into the river from the swamp, likewise Lethe Crick on the east, which borders the Ehrend Furnace Company town-ship, as it is called by the roustabouts of this region.

Here the foundry and general iron-works are housed in long structures of clap-board, shored up with native stone, and bearing high tin roofs. Smoking iron chimblies abound with the same regularity as drunken German, Irish, and Cornish diggers from the coal and iron mines all about.

The local militia-men from the stockade fort built to guard those workers more than like toss half their number through the revolving door of the gaol-house, conveniently enough situated nearest twixt two public houses, the American Hotel and Demetrios Tsarouhas's taverna.

The canal is the newest suitor this cut-purse hamlet seeks to woo, and even some so-called visionary free-thinkers like Mr. Douglas, the one whose eldest carries a rifle for the local militias, or the engraver Mr. Severin, who paints land-scapes and smokes hasheesh and talks of making Rock Springs the pearl of the New World.

Such men have put forth the proposition that perhaps a donkey-railroad, of like kind to those in English collieries, be employed to transport goods as far west as we may yet. I know not of such futures.

The past hath cut my ham-strings, and I must fresco the cell walls with this istoria, this elogium. To the last, my pen shall fly. I know what awaits. It is mine to know. It makes no odds, not any longer.

At the formation of Callaight County, as Rock Springs is being made the seat of justice in this strange, savage land, it is a village of perhaps six hundred houses in the main with few public buildings besides the American Hostel, Piper's Inn, and the several little taverni down in the Furnace district.

The county fair is usually held near Ehrend Furnace on Mr. Douglas's fairgrounds, where he talks of putting in a horse-racing course one day soon. Mr. Douglas founded, and funds, Rock Springs's very first local school-house and brings students from as far as fifteen miles away, the de facto border of the new district.

Until three years ago, the American Hostel, a house of spirits and bawds (and a Jewish one) was designated the site of county courts until L'Enfant's folly was done enough to work in! (They'd tried to put up a hall of justice for courts and jails down-in-town before that. The first board frame burnt flat. No arson was ever proved, though members of that troglodyte Johnnie Mallory's local posse comitatus still have their ideas.)

Goodman Douglas also funds the town library, which operates at present in the back rooms of the towne hall (though as everywhere else, talk of expansion smokes in the pipe of legend). The library is open to the general populace within normal hours of business. *(To read some of their tomes requires a bribe. I've read them all.)*

The new courthouse is located in the centre of Adams Avenue on the north side of Main Street. It was laid out by a visiting architect, Pierre L'Enfant, a gentle young man often seen in the company of General Washington, who spirited him away from that endeavor to design the new capital farther south, on the Potomac.

Excavation of the county courthouse began seven years ago with Bradleigh Matthias and Yuri Nafziger supervising a crew of twenty men, who consumed three hog's heads of beer per day, five such per night, and laid in enough blasting powder to render two local septuagenarians stone deaf, not that either had long to go.

Those roustabouts built their Gobbelin Castle, the true mad-house in stone, right into the slope of the street: three storeys high on both faces, topped by a tall belfry with a half-tonne copper bell, donated by Ehrend Foundry, to call together people for court, church, or to arms.

The courthouse structure is just done with the clock tower and third floor, and a carillon with clockwork mannikins of the arts of civilization to dance on tracks around the widows' walks! (Folly, I tell you. The work will never be completed. The hill-folk shall merely one day shoot them all down like skeet.)

Roughly one mile west of the Diamond is the stockaded block-house of the Rock Springs garrison of the United States Army, on the hill overlooking this very mad-house. Sugar Mill Stream flows westward past the fort with the mouth joining Despond Crick flowing north.

Although not lying on the Jenuchshadaga Indian Trail itself, Rock Springs is only a stone's throw away from that warpath used by all of the Six Nations, until

[indecipherable squiggle]

A noise outside.

Sweet Iesu, the lunatics have forc'd th'door

[fragment is missing]

GANG OF FOUR ORIGINS

2400 Earth CE

He hauled fifty civs out of that tunnel, all told. Fifty casualties spared for Shang 2 and the courage to defend what they had because of what they were. He nearly broke his back and did something to lumbar vertebra #4, which would probably take a regrow to fix, as well as one torn left ACL, a concussion, and numerous supporting cast.

The big male nurse, Nick Coppersmith, got them out. But he heard the rest screaming. The ones he couldn't find and put on his back.

He heard them at night when it was hot. He heard them in the flames, wherever there was fire. He heard them in the dark times, when he couldn't hold it together. He heard them just fine. He was fine. Fine.

That's just what he told Sonia. Fine. He was. Fine. He lost his cushy desk at the Ministry of Rebuilding three weeks after his medical discharge. Called the regional manager a cocksucker and punched his lights out cold. People applauded. But that didn't buy diapers or fuse shut the fingernail lacerations in his cheeks when he got home.

He went to a witch. He went to the village shrink. They both told him the same thing: digest it. Eat the horrid meal trapped halfway down your throat, so you can sick it back up and get the death all out of you. Look at the end of your spoon. Look at the rest of your life. Your. Fucking. Life.

Your life. He hadn't seen Katie since she was a year and a half old—and paid the Imperium a hefty fine for the privilege. Nina claimed domestic abuse, something she knew a lot about. He never hit her. He could never let her have the satisfaction of that. He was an internalizer, the village shrink told him. He kept everything inside until it poisoned him from the fallout.

Until he was re-enlisting, preferring the frying pan. Until he caught himself back in the induction center and wondered why in the hell he was going around and around in the same loop like a lab rat, like . . .

"Like it's the only safe thing left," Nick muttered there in that cold cinderblock bunker and got to his feet, naked as the day he was born, covered in Celtic tribal tattoos across the right side of his body.

His eyes twinkled. "Research and Development, like I heard about . . ."

Long might he have lived to think so.

Recovered Fragment, quarto edition, appears unfinished.
1842 *begun* [sic]; date of assembly uncertain.

Pennsylvania Collection; Letters
CD 18:B: Pre-1860 Americana, Rock Springs
Callaight County Library
Dr. Cricket Bennigan, orig. Redactor

(from) THE TOWN AT THE END OF THE WORLD

Dr. Chambers, Josephus S., III, *Phantasmagoria Weekly*,
Satire Editor At Large
New York City, Manhattan, Broad Way

Just thirty miles north by northwest of the geographical centre of the great State of Pennsylvania, Powersburg lies at the tip of the principal range of the Allegheny Mountains, near the headwaters of the far-famed Monongahela River and on the main line of the Pennsylvania Railroad.

On the left bank of the Bull's Crick branch of the beautiful Monongahela is situated the borough of Powersburg, founded by those pioneers and daring frontiersmen Nathan and William Powers. For years, this metropolis was the business center of what is now Callaight County. It has been the seat of justice since the county's formation.

Geographically, it is located in the northern part of Callaight Township, somewhat south of the center of the county. It was organized as a borough in 1832 but never elected any borough officers after the year of its incorporation, letting its municipal organization die. It has been figured since then as a village, though having over 1,500 in population.

Nathan and William Powers were brothers and natives of the north of Ireland from which they came in 1750 to settle first in Lancaster County, which they soon left on account of the bitter feuds existing between the German and Irish settlers of that county, to trap furs in the Cumberland Gap.

They served in the French and Indian war and marched with Gen. Armstrong to Council Bluffs. The name of the Monongahela who guided Nathan and

William's wonderful way across those snow and ice-covered mountains was one Paul Ross, in the white man's tongue, though the popular local folktale tells us it was the great trickster-hero Crookstaff of the local Irrakwa himself.

Being frontiersmen and war profiteers, Ross and the Powers brothers decided to push further westward and, on their way to cross the Alleghenies, stopped at the site they named Rock Springs, where Nathan Powers was so favorably impressed with the countryside (and shotgun-wed to a fellow trapper's daughter, according to local apocrypha) that he decided to settle down there and prevailed upon his brother William to do the same.

It is a matter of some dispute as to where Paul Ross's original cabin stood. Griff Woodcock's *Architectural History of Callaight County* points the original Powers cabin near the present American Hotel and Public House at the tail tip of Wain Alley one block from the jail; Reifsteck's work claims that it stood on the southwest corner of Main and Adams where the Chang Apothecary presently resides.

Powersburg, which lies just across the river from its own original settlement, is partly on the land taken up by William Powers in 1758. The town was laid out some time before the building of the Erie Canal, pleasantly located on bottom lands.

Powers's heirs owned the land until the building of the canal, when it passed into the virtual control of other parties, and a great lawsuit followed in which the young senator Thaddeus Stephens was conspicuous as an attorney for one of the contesting parties.

At the top of Locke Mountain, one gets a glorious view, spanning miles: a view of the city scattered at one's feet, its houses spread over two narrow strips of ground on the slopes of a broad, vast valley. The railroad compounds and militia bases are strung through the centre in daisy chains.

In 1833, Penn's Grays (organized October 8, 1820) were the first militia of Powersburg, to be closely followed by Sollenheim's Red Caps, garrisoned at the Point of No Return ("up the mountain," to use the quaint nimrod speech of the local hill folk).

The Grays were succeeded by the Monongahela Rifles, which were hastily mustered in 1858 at the direction of Captain John Brown, 125th New York. (Of the Red Caps, not much pertinent information is available.)

The Monongahela Rifles became Company C of the 6th Pennsylvania infantry during the early war, which served in the Army of the Potomac. Under the old militia system of the original Pennsylvania Commonwealth Structure, which was used until a recent date, two weekly encampments were made at Powersburg: the first one of nine companies, commencing October 21, 1812, and the second of seventeen companies, commencing November 1, 1851.

Far away to the south lies the dark-green ridge known as Poe Mountain. The notch in the middle of Poe Mountain is familiarly known by older natives as the Devil's Hemp Yard. Through that notch, the bystander can see the distant slope of more mountains along the Allegheny Ridge proceeding further north.

Such is Powersburg: the distant bell and whistle and the long lines of smoke far down in the valley below, telling of the railroad that has brought the future to this wild land. The growth of Powersburg from a hamlet to an important city has been terminal.

The first building on the site of the town was the old Powers farmhouse. The very next one was a small engineer's office and milking shed. In 1851, there were less than a dozen buildings about the place.

Among them were the Catholic church and school building, the Company, Lusardi's and Schweickart's stores, a lawyer's office, Dr. Holton II's residence, the American Hotel, and a brick building in the course of erection on Virginia Street.

The dream of empire is taking on reality here. The blind Monongahela dragon-goddess Alleghenia will sometimes lavish her favors for hundreds of men without money, but brighter intellects and nobler impulses than were ever possessed have gone down to the grave "unwept, unhonored, and unsung" in this valley as well.

Neither will the soughing of the west wind, as it sweeps through with its aboriginal significance, disturb their repose any more than it will that of the Titans when resting from "life's fitful fever" in their splendid mausoleums.

Powersburg seems to have grown but very slowly from 1790 to 1814. The American Hotel and Public House was a favorite resort as early as 1800. There is dispute as to what year Rock Springs village was completed. Woodcock claims that it was plotted as early as 1780.

In 1814, both towns contained a mere total of eight full-sized buildings: the original mission-church, the American, John Powers's tavern, Griff Woodcock's house, a store, a smitty, the log house of trapper Christian Schmidt, and the first house of town, built by Nathan Powers. By 1829, there were over twenty resident families.

Fast friend of the turnpike was Mr. Blair Callaight of Callaight Gap to the far north. His influence was used in the halls of the legislature until his wife's disgrace injured his political standing. Nevertheless, Callaight persevered until the company was chartered, and he soon had the satisfaction of seeing the Pike Road completed.

The pioneer physician was Dr. Holton, who came in 1789, and the first lawyer was DJ Hohenzollern. The pioneer hotel keeper was Avram Zlotchin, who opened the American Hotel in 1799. Dr. Holton was a practicing physician in Dysart Gap Township, succeeded in 1789 by Dr. John Buchanan, whose successor was Dr. Holton II.

Drs. James Gerraughty, Aethena Dively, and Chadwick Halbritter were practicing out in the townships before 1830. Rock Springs City, so called in its earliest day by its original proprietors, is one of the comparatively new towns in the central part of the state and is in nearly every respect what may be called a "railroad town," owing as Powersburg does its prosperity to the Pennsylvania Railroad's northern line.

Town proper was originally laid out by Messrs. Ehrend, Burkhauser & Co., an old and much respected iron firm that until a few years since carried on extensive ironworks in different parts of the state.

Of these, Gustav Ehrend, a highly respected citizen of the town, assisted in planning the streets and laying out the lots. Ehrend was then the ironmaster of what was known as the Rock Springs Kilns.

In 1813, a land company made up of Messrs. Blair Callaight Jr. and Harald Sveen, Esq, a local entrepreneur, on their way west, were induced to interrupt their journey and look at this new town in the wilderness. The investors were so favorably impressed that they purchased lots and ever afterward identified themselves with the growth and prosperity of Powersburg.

Mr. Callaight died about a year ago, after being widely and favorably known over the entire state as an active and honorable businessman. He was president of the Callaight County Banking Company at the time of his demise. Mr. Sveen commenced in the apothecary business, in which he is still engaged. Mr. Callaight (now passed on to his rewards) started in hemp farming and retired a very rich man.

Then came time to build the Main Line Canal along the Monongahela River.

This was soon followed by the PRR Northern railroad line over the Allegheny Mountains to connect the land to the visionary era of "flush times" when vast sums of money were won or lost and property along the river suddenly quadrupled in value. These were "Legerdemain times."

On the morning of April 20, 1859, the town was visited by a terrible storm and flood. The rain began falling around midnight and continued in unceasing torrents until about six o'clock in the morning. The waters descended furiously in every direction from the high grounds until all that portion of Lower Heaven Hill Road, lying between the railroad and the river, was in fact underwater.

The Monongahela River had risen about twenty feet above her ordinary level. Nearest the river, the water in the dwellings and shops rose as high as eight feet. Much devastation was wrought on the canal between Powersburg and Erie.

The Council Bluffs Reservoir was built in 1840 by Oscar J. Paterson. His previous attempt, at a now-undisclosed location, soon found to be infested with a predatory freshwater amphibian of a type previously unknown and quickly made extinct in the name of all that decency upholds.

These "Yankee gators" quickly passed into the stuff of legend, though a certain kind of upright-walking salamander has passed into quaint local tall-tale. (***reference, "Moeb Lizard," index. Cross-ref: Catty Wampus, Hugag, Hoop Snake, Mountain-Turkey, Sidehill Gouger, &c.)

The present reservoir, with a three-million-gallon capacity, was then erected one hundred twenty feet in elevation above all points in the city. The town was ignited by gas in 1852, and the Edison Company of New York plans to electrify the area entirely soon when adequate hydro-electric dams can be constructed on the Monongahela; the first of many are already underway.

The Edison Electric Light Company was organized here in 1856 with limited service to the hinterlands and motors supplied from the Callaight Heat, Light, and Power Company, which was equipped with four thousand Edison lamps.

The electricity has its plant on 10th Avenue. Had anyone predicted electrification or an event of its kind some years back, they in all probability would have been burned as a wizard or set down as deranged and thrown in Demarest. There are those who still would argue favorably upon the matter.

Transportation too knows few fences here. Powersburg is the nexus of the new transcontinental railroad, and the PRR knew what they were doing when they located here along the southwestern Erie Mainline Canal in 1845. The railroad divides east from west here, states from territories, civilization from

savagery. Pittsburgh only became the Iron City a few years later. Powersburg
left the lamp burning for her.

When the railroad first went through Rock Springs, new homes cropped up
like mushrooms on both sides of the tracks. Today the railroad slices the city
neatly in half. The PRR employs about 5,000 men now. They will soon be able
to build many hundred locomotive engines yearly. Their continued operation
will doubtless exponentiate Powersburg's population.

The PRR shop complex has spread from its humble beginnings to cover much
of West Indian Valley, in the area known to local itinerants as the Loop, from
Dysart on the northeast to South Crestview on the southwest. The New York
Southern and Western Railroad, newly chartered, is planned to give all New
York rail lines access to our city, including the Port Authority Cannonball, all
the way south to University Park.

The new railroad will run from Powersburg to Point of No Return over the
Frankstown Pass, and from that point will extend to Ringler's Corners. The road
will be electrified and will also be fitted for steam traffic.

Point of No Return is one of the oldest towns in the county, being laid out
about 1793 or 1794. It is on Poplar Run Road in Callaight Township, four miles
southwest of Powersburg, and is the present terminus of the Point of No Return
spur of the Pennsylvania Railroad.

Its founder, Travis Weyandt, was a native of Croyon. At an early day, Point of
No Return was an active business center on the Old Pike Road, but its progress
was checked by the growth of Powersburg and the travel on the canal.

With the building of the K-666 branch of the Pennsylvania Railroad, the
town received a new impetus and promises to become a place of importance.
The destruction of the Old Canal and the dissolution of the Ringler's Corners
Brick Manufacturing Company affected the prosperity of the village for some
years, and its surrounding hamlets of Alleghenia, Spring Dam, and Blackbird
Pie.

One hundred twenty-two acres of town are occupied by the Pennsylvania
Railroad Company. The upper shops are machine shops while the lower are the
car shops, presided over directly by master mechanic Thomas K. Montgomery,
all located in the triangular plot of ground slightly south of Our Lady of the
Alleghenies churchyard on the 1200 block of Grant Street.

At the car shops, extending from 29th to 40th Streets, passenger touring cars
are built and custom-designed for performers such as the novelty act Bridget

Lemere, the Kootenai Princess, an Iroquoian chanteuse who opened for the Swedish Nightingale at the Orpheum Theatre last October.

Trains at every hour of day and night arrived and departed from Powersburg in the early days under the supervision of the late Professor Casey Jones, trainmaster, one of the most efficient railway men in the state. A perfect system prevails past the professor's demise. Passengers and freight are speedily handled without confusion or mistake. PRR-funded work has already been started to convert Point of No Return into a summer resort such as is found in the east. For years, Lakeside Park, three miles from the city, has been classed among the finest summer resorts in the country, and for years to come will likely be one of the city's most popular breathing spots.

The City Passenger Railway Company of Powersburg (operated by electricity) was incorporated March 10, 1852. The first electric cars were run July 4 that year. The line now extends from the Monongahela to the city line at 1st Street. The Chestnut Avenue A branch, operated by horse power, extends from 17th Street to 25th Street. Other branches are in construction.

The Powersburg & Point of No Return railroad furnishes rapid and comfortable transit to and from Powersburg. From the top of Poe Mountain on the railway line, looking south and east, Powersburg can be seen very distinctly, Dysart more distant, and an extensive panorama of hill and valley, cleared field, and woodland dell discernible for five counties.

The average amount paid to the railroaders of Powersburg alone each month is over one million dollars. This creates healthy growth and permanent business for the Ehrend Company Stores. Powersburg is the logical trade centre of all Central Pennsylvania, and the merchants and businessmen are gradually extending their activities to the surrounding districts with our kind governor's latitude.

The citizenship is of the highest grade to be found anywhere. The railroad has donated hundreds of thousands of dollars to the school shop courses. Trade teaching receives unusual attention. Graduates of Kirke School and Our Lady of the Alleghenies parochial school are later committed to the most prestigious institutions of higher learning on the strength of their diplomas.

Powersburg is also home to St. Basil's Jesuit University, which has survived at the former St. Basil's Monastery in several incarnations since 1809. Houses of public worship dot every corner with all conceivable denominations well represented. The city is the Episcopal seat of the Roman Catholic diocese of

Powersburg, and there is even a Freedman's Baptist Church on 18th Street!

Seven-Mile Lake, upon being entirely completed at its scheduled date of May 15, 1864, will have cost a tiny fraction of the amount which has been spent on the endless miles of the roads. The trolley and local rail system is one of the best in the nation, its new spurs in view and projected to extend everywhere.

Most of the city and some of the hamlets now have electric lighting as do a few surrounding hamlets. Electricity can be delivered cheaply straight from the Monongahela River from the hydro-electric dams at Council Bluffs, scheduled for completion very soon.

The Monongahela shops turn out heavy locomotives used on the railroad for passenger and freight traffic. Their facility boasts the largest locomotive roundhouse in the world, in addition to its repair shops. At Ringler's Corners are the vast PRR foundries where brass and soft iron equipment and wheels are turned out. A new roundhouse, turntable, coal-tip, and repair shop are to be put into place at the Monongahela Shops upon completion of the underground spur of the Callaight County Trolley Line.

The machinery and gear maintained in these various shops, to say nothing of the men who run the works, guarantee that the quality of work generated is unsurpassed, down to the thousands of well-paid clerks and railroaders who see Powersburg as their true home.

Among the more prominent events in the history of Powersburg may be mentioned the railroad-iron war at the Ehrend Foundry in 1854, among the Irish laborers employed there, which was suppressed without loss of life by the Powersburg guards and hired agents of the Pinkterton Detective Agency.

The iron manufactories of Powersburg were inaugurated in 1789 when Gus Ehrend and others built Powersburg Furnace No. 1. The Powersburg Iron Company has a large rolling mill just south of the city limits on the Powersburg branch of the Pennsylvania Railroad, Main Street Station, where all kinds of merchant bar iron are manufactured.

They were first built in 1848, were burned down May 23, 1854, but at once re-built, and the company is now in a very flourishing condition. The paper mill, which is often operated day and night, is the sole industry of Croyon. It is one of the most complete paper manufactories in the state, and its extensive machinery is run automatically by a mammoth Babbage sorting-engine which

(continues next page)

GANG OF FOUR ORIGINS

2400 Earth CE

Cathy Two Blades had just lost sight of her mother when the jelly mine made landfall twenty feet ahead of her. Mama had the morphia syrettes. That was bad. All Cathy had now was the pain.

She couldn't make her left eye do anything, no matter how much she tried to blink. And the total darkness thing kinda sucked too. So did not being able to move her arms or legs. Oh, it was just one goddamned malfunction after another.

The left eye. The ex-eye. The black wing of her hair hissing over the socket like tiny wire whips through Cathy's soul. That one other thing she couldn't think about. Because she was going to have to think about it. She took a hard hit on the left side of the face, and the eye was the least of her worries. Most known of her quantities. Nonexistent, and screaming its new absence in pain that would cash in its real chips later. The journey to that point in time sounded like a strange, brutal trip. A short one from now that would take forever. And hurt. For. Ever.

WHUP. WHUP. WHUP. Updrafts beneath mighty pinfeathers, pinions, catching drag, thrust, circling. The mighty wings of the thunderbird Deathmother, forever circling the globe, landing . . . landing . . . black feathers circled in the air about her head, diving in closer, closer—

Cathy heard the Deathmother's song, the beaksounds sharpening knives that cut holes in the sky for the keening choirs of exterminating angels raised in hymns to bloody slaughter. Crowsong and crowbarsong, boots stomping skulls in the frozen light of war. Deserters treading the boards of the world stage for the last time, the trick trapdoor beneath their feet that cracks into the morning light as babies crown who'll one day hang someone else . . .

Her very small voice. Littlegirlvoice. LittlehidingCathyvoice. "Take me home, Mama. Take me home. Please. Oh, this eye. Mama, I ain't scared. Just please."

WHUP. WHUP. WHUP. Just the sound of the Deathmother's wings. Circling, circling. With little Cathy beneath them, circling . . .

Back. The snap and boom of landing in her body, the smoke from the tunnel, the bright bursts of fire.

By the time the medic, whose battle-buddies called him Sundevil, hauled her out of Hill 19—the highway-bridge settlement in the area that used to be called Powersburg—Cathy was raving prayers to Raven and the Baby Jesus, weaving one into the other as all things do, one into the other, all stories into the greater cloth.

The chirurgiens did what they could about the pain on the long ride to the shore. The glass eye she chose was solid black, and that was good because there happened to be two just like it. Spares. Cathy paid for all three with her dead mother's money. Mama, a trained nurse, would in fact have demanded it.

The wisewoman who prepared her eye socket was also a tattooist. Her family came from Ni-Hon, in the Ago, and Saori had hammers and little needlepoint things, and it all sounded like music, down to the way she talked the whole way through setting the living coral in Cathy's eye and leaving it to grow.

Music. Saori was chattering about the Deathmother from the word go. Saori saw things. Things other people didn't know they projected. Raven's wing was tattooed across Cathy's left cheek, down from the hairline. Gorgeously. (Soon enough, a camera was ingrown. But not just then.)

GANG OF FOUR CODA

THE STARS DON'T LEAD BACK HOME

At every point in Time, then and now, andwhen and elsewhen and otherwhen, even with long, long hindsight, when the Peacemaker blew and the horrible thing happened, none of the so-called "Gang of Four" really knew where the hole had started. Some unshielded micron of crystal touching some bead of vat-grown solder, missed in some fractional nanomoment of hurry by the probing eyes of Mara-Sam's tech squadrons.

Some breach in the mags somewhere, some effect with someone's name that Coppersmith, in his mad exuberance, failed to clear with the group or was too strung out himself to apprehend . . .

"Or something I missed. O Lord, something I did or failed to do. Jesus our savior, forgive me and my fellows, for we know not what we did. We tried, Lord. We tried to help. We just wanted to help . . ."

Or so went the terrified thoughts of Cathy Two Blades, nurse to herself and the rest of them, standing behind the big holopane monitor as her old friend Eddie Donnellaigh made his big speech that was the last thing any of the four scientists remembered for quite a while, just before the hole opened under the city, and they were suddenly somewhere else.

They all remembered Eddie's speech, the one that played on every pane in the Sacred City of Shang 2—above ground, below ground, in orbit—when it happened, the day everything went to hell. Again.

They all remembered the way his left eye was twitching, and his knobby little old-man hands were drumming the arms of his chair. "Every design has a flaw," the senior researcher of Emperor Marek Demarest's brain trust thundered in his still, slight brogue. "We folk of true science, both hereabout and planetwide, these days, have beaten war machines into geosynchronous orbiters and our interstel craft. Such as they have found. Such as they have brought back and done so far and will do still more . . . with . . . more . . . effort . . ."

A hitch in his voice, a sense of crazed desperation, nobility. A twinkle on the ancient spectacles clipped to his bulbous nose. "We have found and learned to communicate with our dear Guardians, the silicate-based organisms with which we have shared the earth for unknown epochs. With their invaluable minds, their undying love, we have exponentiated the organic-computing abilities of the human brain tenfold with the headgear they taught us to grow and the bonding they share with those most gifted of our children, once Kybernoidia and now by their own designation . . . *hrrump* . . . the Illegitimi."

Cathy Two Blades remembered the little old man peering around at them all, eyes as serious as Death. She thought of the Deathmother, circling the globe and never touching down. Where the shadow of her wing touched land . . .

"But we canNOT. FIX. EVERYTHING."

Universes were born and died in the pregnant silences between his syllables. "Today, we join with our kinfolk around the globe to usher in a new age of cheap, clean, endless power through this noble device that all our hands made and all will defend in the knowledge that the Singularity Generator"—he gave an indulgent, condescending chuckle—"as the wags call it in the news these days, will in fact now and forever eliminate conflict—"

That voice was the last thing the Four heard for a while, that voice and the creaking of old Donnellaigh's chair that kept the war-mangled stumps of his legs a foot above the fused-stone floor.

Then every monitor in the arena glowed in a different light. A jaundiced, rippling light, but the face on every screen was the same. A mosaic that made a whole. If you could call it that. A *hole*.

A profile like a thumb and forefinger poised to pinch. The nose growing, the chin rising to meet it, the teeth sharpening, rotting. Even those changes had just begun.

"Sic semper tyrannis," was all the new face said.

And then—

Famous last words. But now the hole in the air above the Peacemaker, the little door, had been contained and harnessed. In their silvery workshells, with their

multiplicities of identical appendages, the Guardians threw a field over it and routed their own instruments through that field. Threading the hole.

The Guardians, with what knowledge they were able to piece together, were still trying to get objects through said hole when the one man they wanted least to know about it volunteered to be first in line to go through himself.

The emperor was hospitalized. After his son, the lineage was hopelessly snarled. Yet Lt. Taliesn Demarest, Illegitimi-Alpha Class, said son, chose to be first in line for his city, for his dear Maeve, for his own sanity.

(Or so he told himself at the time. The first attempt went too fast. Left him with an entire Purgatory in which to repent. More or less literally . . .)

On and on, beneath the city of Shang 2, the Peacemaker howled with cosmic dissonance. The hole that tore the air above it wide open was still there but pulsing randomly now, the way it had been when the Terrible Thing happened. Now it was bright, shimmery, opalescent.

On and on, the Peacemaker whined beneath the city. Four humans in the whole teeming megalopolis of Shang 2 had designed the thing, and only those four knew exactly how to shut it off. And they were gone. A long, long way from home.

On and on, the mile-wide circumference of the perpetual accelerator rang, still out of tune, beneath the city in the oldest and dirtiest original quarters, far under a mountain that was so built upon that very few people remembered it was a mountain at all—once called the Mountain of Sorrows.

Only the Four held within each of their precisely augmented brains exactly one-quarter of the deactivation code, no more. Protocol, as ever it had been. None of them could have imagined what happened.

But all of them should have seen it coming.

Duh.

The Terrible Thing happened. It was still happening. But it was harnessed now, tapped into. The Guardians figured that riff out in about five seconds. No matter what the medium, a hole was a hole.

You could send a plumb bob down a hole, even one of their own mechanized species nutty enough or far along enough in their own life not to care if they came back.

It self-identified as male. His name was Mandelbrot, and for years, he'd been a hero of his tribe.

They could map this hole in everything that their toy had made when the rogue kid, the *other* Demarest brat, jacked it up and turned it on. They could go in first, they reasoned, without any actual-fully-fledged city Illegitimi volunteering to become human spaghetti at either end, in sloppy emulation of their more-evolved teacher.

But even the Guardians couldn't control the hole the Peacemaker made in everything. And then Typhon Demarest walked through, raising both middle fingers in the supercooled air.

Typhon Demarest, with the jaundice he got shooting gods-knew-what-all in his veins, the Hepatitis K or whatever the fuck his irredeemable, illegitimately Illegitimus-gifted ass was up to now after how many tens of tries to clean up: the hard time in Juvie, the thalamic lock, the diencephalic inhibitor. The meds. The exile. The . . . all the rest.

Typhon Demarest, chewing up every screen in Shang 2 . . . forever. The hole could get bigger at any time with different currents that carried different consequences.

Still, in time, all lessons prove themselves.

BOOK 1: ALPHABET OF LIGHTNING

DEPRESSION-FLOWERS

May 15, 1927

The stone stretch of Route 30 is foregrounded by sooty coal smoke rising from the hills, crematoriums for the dinosaurs, gnome torches from burrows at the roots of the mountains.

The bombed, homely face of Powersburg, Pennsylvania drools glittering coal oil and old yellow light. It is the face of a hard past full of broken homes and toys and bones, an open sulfur-cured wound in the earth, the scab gone Halloween orange.

Skeletal hands jitter at radio dials all over town, searching for a brighter frequency through scrambling layers of steel and rotting linoleum that choke out the signals from anywhere else. Psalms sung bloody-black-and-blue shush its nightly screams, narcotized by the hazy glow of streetlights the same shade as the sulfurous creeks from the strip mines on Locke Mountain's west face.

Funny, hollow-eyed children stare at newcomers in the streets, their gaze parting cobwebs of memory, searching for some justification of their own existence. In every stranger's face, they see a liberator, a young, crewcut Christ to dig up their battered hearts from the backyard. Orange tears burn on their faces as they turn and walk the other way at your puzzled look.

What a strange creature has been allowed to evolve to such an age, decanted from the oldest of bottles to sear the tissues like Médoc and mustard gas, chlorine canisters exploding upwind, burning a vomitous hole in the throat. Wind whistles through the woods, singing songs of random deaths and accidents and pockets full of money. Singing songs of the land, broken into bits and burned in the stove, generating fibrous tumors of human civilization against the skin of reality.

The chemicals in the earth have mummified the past. The burning golden future seethes outside the horizon like a John Milton monster rally beyond the flat edge of the known world.

Beneath the killing wilderness surrounding town on all four sides, mine tunnels wend their way in crumbling wasp nests, hither and yon. Every now and then, a street collapses, entire abandoned blocks immolated in random implosion. People rarely notice.

Rivers of ooze flow on through all those years of empty promises. The hollow-eyed kids dig for miracles in the hills, finding nothing but bones and clinkers from the Civil War days, now and then a croaker marble or two, or a musket ball.

The rock dumps. Back in the woods, butted up against the foothills. Looming over them.

A million tons of slag torn from the tunnels and strip mines all around that clear-cut, blasted heath on the west face of the known world. The miners call the stuff "bony," and there are indeed plenty of bones buried there from days just dead, when Mollie Maguire was queen of the tunnels and the White Lotus Union shut down the rail shops.

Look well upon this land. Trace the trapped flow of the swamp where prehuman foundations sank beneath the bedrock long ago, hinting at a "someday" that never came, choked by careless chemicals down into the ooze. Behold the sunlight that cracks on the surface of streams in the woods, and the towering slag heaps at the foot of the mountain on the back side where most folks don't go.

The land around the rock dumps is a prehistoric seabed. It makes the very flesh hiss with all those lies burned into one—from birth around here—in the water we drink, the air we breathe, and all that manages to survive in the waste dump that spawned us.

The rock dumps glow at night, crackling orange with the bones of scabs and miners and lynched John Henrys, burning from the compacted pressure of all that weight and coal on itself. When it rains, the steam is enough to knock the feathers off an eagle.

The bones of striker and strike-breaker alike still burn in those bony piles, compacted into diamonds long ago, dug up and carved away a piece at a time to be sold as relics to the Church, or as fuel or fill for that new state highway out of town they never finished.

The gnomes are all gone from that groaning ground, for the day. The machinery has fallen silent. All that remains are the cries of mutant birds and the endless lapping of the crick at your back. Islands within it still yield archaeological records of a mineral boom that is burning itself out even now, with only fallout to remain.

And if you listen late at night, you can hear the land screaming in its sleep.

For one second, dreaming of that place, that ancient Powersburg place, Taliesn Demarest, the scar-faced prodigal brat of a lame-duck emperor, an upstart prince who sailed around death, hung over the earth in blinding cold so vast he couldn't speak, clouds drifting across the Peruvian highlands far down and to the left, the Andes a big, swollen scar . . .

Then Taliesn was being born again, into a new year, a new name, and the blind dragon-goddess Alleghenia cackled from her crystal sepulcher to hear Prince Tally yanked once more from the Dream . . .

Legends. Prophecies. Dreams. After a while, it's only so much paper.

But oh, all those poems lost in the rushes, the screeds of a boy who could draw lightning, written in that painful, crabbed hand, loaded down as both of Shamus Connelly's poor hands were, with their freight of extra fingers and weird hollow bones full of coal and toxic metals . . . hands full of stories that never made it anywhere, yellowed in composition notebooks, unwept, unhonored, unsung, waiting.

Waiting to blow in a rice-paper wind back along the street, filling the Town at the End of the World with a time that once was. The clouds grind overhead. The Victrola needle falls, and the song spins right up.

Breezy draughts soaked with the sage-and-honey smell of the woods around the river, down at the bottom of Grant Street, drifting toward the top where the Connellys' old brick house with the cupola rises from the dead-end corner of the block. The copper lightning rod at the cupola's tip is built into the frame, already bitter green with rain.

The breeze flows through the window screen, under the door, cooling their burning faces, carrying an electric chorus of crickets through the vast night.

The young city of Powersburg hangs in the great, hazy cobweb of stars at the wall of Sleep, at the borderland of Dream, in a foggy valley at the edge of a vast, poisoned marsh. The picket fence that makes good neighbors here is hewn of cow horns and elephant tusks. Past its swinging graveyard gate lies madness. Welcome home.

When he was a boy, in the Irish shantytowns of the Thornley coalfields, Joe Connelly's father taught him to make what would later come to be called Depression-flowers. You pour iodine, merthiolate, merbromin, and ammonia over a bowl full of coal, and crystals grow straight up from the raw carbon—

The lightning hits the house at the moment of conception, of silence between inhale and exhale, of sharp, startled shock as the lovers come to climax together, looking at each other with new eyes for just a moment.

It flickers like a magic lantern between them, like a stereopticon, like a motion picture, fading on their eyelids in stark blacks and whites.

Powersburg, Pennsylvania.

The house shakes, crockery rattling in every cupboard. A tremendous *whackKOW* rolls and rumbles off through the night. Tomorrow, Joe and his brothers will rip the shingles and flashing off that section of roof that was destroyed by the lightning.

Say the name, and feel your mind stretch through stagnant seas of gossip, through immigrations and emigrations and migrations and random deaths on the back pages of the Sentinel . . .

When in their cups later, the brothers will learn just *what* Joe was up to when the lightning struck. The roar of approval will ring as old as time (from those hell-burnt Geordies whose idea of dressing down is to remove their jackets whilst digging a septic tank in some relative's or neighbor's backyard, men who work so hard in the nine-to-seven that to do such a thing seems a wee bit of fun in the off hours) . . .

Fall through miles of newspaper-morgue microfilm, reeling along loopy, old wax library-phonograph blanks, the hissing phantom voices haranguing phantom crowds, drunk as skunks under the grandstand on the courthouse lawn, while a fiddle pierces the still air from somewhere just outside the pickup of the ancient microphone.

Joe's mind is full of those Depression-flower crystals for some reason, a memory of the back porch of their house in another land, grains of sand, pearls, oysters, irritations . . . the blood, sweat, and tears he and his family had spilled down the side of the coal face, the rock that is Anna, and what fey colors might rise from the face of that rock when the right mix was applied . . .

Joe is lit, bent, out on the piss. He won't remember these thoughts as he is asleep in ten seconds . . . though such thoughts once drove him to write verse he never showed anyone. No verse in the mines that he'd come to tolerate and then to love and then to hate, unable to escape . . .

His thoughts are mostly of sleep and that he has to get to work by five. If he were sober, he'd remember that the Carlton Company was still laying men off. He couldn't go back down to the mine office for a work ticket until the following Sunday.

There would be a lot of that in the years to come. Joe had mined back home, and now he mined here. It was never so bad back home until the end, and none of these red-capped freaks stealing the coal either. (They had words for them back home too . . .)

So drifting, he rests his head on the shoulder of his fair colleen and falls back to sleep, dreaming of the strange veins of metal in Tunnel 10, and the weird blue lights that go about hither and yon along below, up and down the tunnels like ball lightning on the railroads topside. Like the faeries St. Patrick sent away. Perhaps, Joe often groans, they got sent here.

Anna Connelly sits up in the dark, rolling one of Joe's Bull Durhams. There are two things Joe's good for these days, and a cigarette's the second. "Like yeh'd mind, yeh big stupid git. Connelly, if it weren't for the brain between yer legs, I'd have blown t'other'n out of your head wi'yer own rifle five year ago."

Moodily, she pads out on the screen porch to smoke and see if the lightning hit anything. But she knows it did.

Even before she goes out barefoot in her nightshirt and peers up at the house. She knows that it hit something. This is not good news. But it is.

Inside her, electric telegraphs twitch out a slippery warning, microcosm and macrocosm ringing a five-alarm pregnancy. The babby will be . . .

A priest, something in her hindbrain whispers, but the image that comes to mind is not at all consistent with Church dogma.

A tall young man with red hair and hooded eyes, his kind yet unhappy face wracked with pain as he raises his arms to the sky, tattooed blacksnakes moving along the arms of the new Druid, hissing, the healer's familiars . . .

There's something in the air tonight. Anna's had a few shots of the ould devil whisky as well. They both did. She sits down, closing her eyes and smoking for a while. Letting the fine flash fade . . .

CERTIFICATE OF LIVE BIRTH

Name: Connelly, Shamus Joseph
Date Of Birth: 01 Jan, 1928 Time: 12:01 AM
County Of Birth: Callaight
Place Of Birth: Powersburg, PA
Gender: Male
Race: White
Parent's Residence: Powersburg, PA
Mother's Name: Connelly, Anna Marie Nee Mohanty
Mother's Age: 28
Mother's Birthplace: County Cork, Ireland
Father's Name: Connelly, Joseph Edward
Father's Age: 32
Father's Birthplace: County Sligo, Ireland
Doctor: Johannes Drebel MD
Hospital: MERCY HOSPITAL

NOTES: Infant Connelly, Shamus, displays no signs of idiocy as yet. Parents are good Catholics, so did not wish the child to be [here a line is struck out]. However, skull is large and abnormally shaped with frontal bossing—forehead high and very prominent, no evidence of precocious closure of cranial sutures. Postaxial and preaxial polysyndactyly present: five full supernumerary fingers on each hand apart from normal five, webbed. Second and third toes also syndactyl, also webbed—

The nib of Dr. Drebel's pen rasped across the birth certificate, forever dividing *before* from *after*. He felt and heard the lightning lick the roof *again*.

"This is simply not possible!" he snapped to no one in particular. Every light on the ward flickered and went out. He heard the basement generator lugging to life with a faraway diesel rumble.

For a while, there was only darkness and a fading flash on the old doctor's retinas, an inverse afterimage frozen at the moment of its own formation.

Damn it, this was the third time tonight, the second since he'd come on the ward. He shook his head. *Tch-tch-tch.* Have to say something to Councilman Hoenstine about getting some lightning rods to put on the roof. There'd been a drummer by, selling them just last week. Perhaps he was still in town.

Johannes took a deep breath, trying to still his memories of that poor baby boy. It would be hard for the boy—and for the father and mother. It was hard for him, Johannes, to bite down on his tongue and cut the cord, and the kid was already *looking around* when he did: that *couldn't happen.* He was already reaching out to try to touch something with those . . .

Hands wasn't the word. Johannes didn't have the English. *Appendages. Formations.*

He had to stop there, out of the iron discretion burned into his exhausted brain by the time he finally made it through medical school. Johannes put his pen down and cried. Another poisoned miner's misborn child brought across the river into . . .

"Egypt's land." The pen came back up, clicking against his teeth. "And when the basket was opened, the baby wept . . ."

He was tired. His mind was coughing things out at random. Maybe he'd done right to let the child live, even in this town where such a creature would be hounded to death in minutes by the pecking party of the status quo.

The coal mines in this mountainous part of the world seemed to breed monsters. Most of them never made it out of the operating theater. But once in a while, one did. Those usually stayed at home, but maybe there could be tricks learned, tricks up the sleeve to hide the hands at the ends of them.

When he was an undergrad, Johannes studied Maskelyne and Angier and all the greatest stage magicians. *Perhaps a gaff could be built from ordinary household parts,* he mused, *metal struts from a splint, regular gardening gloves . . .* his brain was already working through the schema. *Plain black leather gloves with springs and struts in each of the primary five fingers . . .*

Perhaps. Johannes decided he'd keep top eye on Shamus for a few years and do what he could to speed that day along. Finishing up his rounds now would bring him that much closer to Sister Marcia down in Emergency. Sister Marcia had an industrial sewing-machine at her disposal and owed him a favor. In his head, Drebel was already tinkering with his next invention.

Just home from the maternity ward, the fair young colleen Anna Connelly held her poor beautiful freak to her breast, and sang him a song as old as the seas that steamed up from the central fire when the continents still slid across the planet . . .

> *Over in Killarney,*
> *Many years ago,*
> *Me mither sang a song to me*
> *In tones so sweet and low . . .*

In his cradle by the fire, baby Shamus stirred in his blankets, cooing at the warmth and the light and the stories played out in the flickering flames.

A pine knot popped in the grate. He tried to clap his hands, but they were swaddled in separate cloths. *Behind his eyes, sparks crossed from pole to pole . . .*

What story does anyone try to tell the world? Triumph. Disgrace. The whole human comedy played out in a little shitpot Pennsylvania mining town on the morning when a Dutch country doctor delivered a ten-pound baby boy with ten fingers and split thumbs on *either* hand, an abnormally large head, and a skeletal structure that required a separate page.

Surely the boy would have to go live with the Sisters and never see the light of day. No town family would—

But Joe and Anna Connelly were far more mismatched than any town family and not thinking right about most things. Since they'd come to America, Joe was a mine foreman, and his blushing bride now helped run the Town Library with honoraria from Holy Mother Church and any other high donors.

Behind his eyes, Shamus Connelly already dreamed and dreamed and dreamed. In his sleep, he suckled milk and grew as strong as Finn M'Coul, if only in his heart, strong as Hercules in the cradle of snakes. He carried his own cradles of snakes at the ends of his wrists, but just then, his poor hands were folded to his chest, and he knew peace.

And I'd give the world if she could sing
That song to me today,
Too-ra-loo-ra-loo-ra . . .
Too-ra-loo-ra-li . . .

Baby Shamus heard her voice, the voice of the Goddess from a towering height, lost in primal mists of the dawn times, the first age of his new world. In his dream, the thundering ocean beat and beat and beat with the tidal roar of the Great Mother's heart.

Too-ra-loo-ra-loo-ra . . .
Oh, hush, now don't you cry . . .

Anna crawled back through the half-doze, back through her mind, back through her own Slough of Despond. She'd come this way again to hold her first child, all this and more. It was worth it now. Maybe just now, but maybe just now was enough . . .

Anna brought the baby home against medical advice to the tune of Joe standing behind her, agreeing for once, "The law of the state be damned. End of the rud, this is."

Joe's face looked old and sorrowful and needing a drink at ten in the morning after three days of waiting at home through Anna's false labor, living on lemon pie filling and potted meat. "Boy stays wi'us . . ."

But in his eyes, Anna could see the trials to come, even before the rest of the blood and neighbor-type family got there. Even before community came rushing back in, community and culture and church and every other set of claptrap, deafening her even in the scant sleep she was ever allowed.

Torrey Skellington, that horrid creature that married Joe's gentle-giant brother Bud, would be giving her three different sets of snide, superstitious-if-not-downright-pagan advice about arcane kills and cures of the newly born. Lena, her other new weird sister-in-law, was a bit more charming and down to earth but dumber than a sack of wet mice.

It was only Paula she truly got on with: Paula the wise bohemian eldest sister who'd been everywhere and done everything, been places and done things that few in Powersburg could even imagine, let alone pronounce, and come back home to put a check rein on the Connelly penny-dreadful drama wherever and whenever possible.

Paula was in the delivery room when Shamus was born and kissed the top of his head like the fairy godmother she occasionally turned out to be anyway for everyone she knew.

No one was a stranger in big sister's house very long. Big sister gave her a knock of brandy in a glass of warm milk just after all that. "No more, or yeh'll put the child off his feed," Paula counseled in that wonderfully gravelly brogue that made Anna think of Mum.

Paula had not peered into said bottle herself once since Anna could remember. She was home from abroad, and no one thought ill of her for putting anything away. Ecclesiastes said there was a time to heal, and that was for everybody. Anna was never from the drinkers though, and that wee draught of brandy put her right out for the next thirteen hours . . .

Days, nights, blurred into weeks of being up like the dead at any un-Christian hour of the clock, the horridness of changing nappies, let alone washing the buggered things in the backyard tub.

Sometimes, Anna Connelly (who had to make herself quit saying Mohanty) wondered if she'd ever sleep again. But all she had to do to get right at that point, every time (when she remembered), was touch the poor webs of bone at the end of her baby boy's wrists, and he would quit blattering, roll over, and go back to sleep.

He was spooky, this wee Shamus, and needed no words to talk. Anna's own inner Slough of Despond was as wide as the cold Atlantic with her own dear dead Mither, Maggie Mohanty, not yet cold in her grave when she took Joe's rough hand and never looked back at that old fieldstone farmhouse that would never truly be a home again with Mama gone and poor Papa grousing himself to bits like the old soldier he would forever be, snapping and snarling at anything that got close.

Anna knew, in the heart-of-hearts where women just know, that she'd also been well and truly drug backways through Joe's own slow mauling by the black dogs of depression and drink when he realized that poverty was an American industry, just as it had been under John Bull back home.

There was a nervous kind of peace now between English-born bride and armed, drunken Irish upstart, a truce at the border that the baby's coming helped to bring about if only for a short while.

The last time Joe hit her was a week before Anna found she'd kindled. She'd "mouthed off," to use Joe's selfish phrase, about some inconsequential thing, and then—

And then it happened. Plato talked about it all coming down to one thing. One separation. The breaking of a stick. Snap. She knew how to read just as well as any girl in her family (even though she liked Diogenes and the Stoics a little better).

"No, by God, you will NOT," the red-headed wildcat rose up righteous and roared, and the hot skillet swung off the stove. It swung the tune without the words, without so much as a potholder or a rag. It swung, and she was death, Death swinging death at the back of his head, and his nose collided with the lip of the kitchen sink on the way down.

Clunk. The sound haunted her dreams for years. Those dreams weren't invariably bad. They just meant something had finished. Always. Just. Finished.

Finished. Anna Connelly was sorry, so sorry she'd done it, instantly, but not as sorry as he was when her Joe finally came home three days later with his nose in a splint and a fistful of roses in one rawboned hand.

Outside the window, the robins had just returned to coal country, and the mountain laurels were blooming in the side yard. Anna just stood and waited, not bothering to stop doing the dishes whilst appraising him, calm and patient as an owl. If she had ever perched with skillet in hand.

Joe never said where the roses came from. He never said much. But that day, he looked her in the eyes out of the one she'd blackened where he hit the sink.

"I went to Confession," he mumbled. "And I confess to you too."

Her split-thumbed hand carved a spiral in the dishwater. "And . . ."

Time stretched out in the kitchen. Joe was miserably sober and talked very fast, and many things got well and truly sorted out before dinner. Many but not enough, just enough to lose track of battles and wars and be done.

He couldn't live much longer anyway, she thought sourly, *not the way he did for himself with the drink.* For that thought, Anna went to Confession herself and tried again. Not in the same bed. But again. She did it anyway. Because she had given her heart to Christ, and if He could take on what He did, then her back could fit this burden.

Anna came out of the memory, her flaxen-haired angel asleep at her breast. She would keep the family together if it killed her for the sake of the child she bore for Joe. If it killed her . . . or him. But never Shamus.

Never her dear little waterhorse, her changeling. She'd stand in the way every time. Joe and his little pet poison priest down at St. Andy's could say all they wanted to about the old tales from home and the like, but her mother told her that the changelings, those that seem to us misborn or feeble, half there or put together wrong, were closest to God.

Now she played with a lock of the baby's amazingly wavy hair. Her hair was that color too, when she was wee, but soon enough coarsened and reddened to the County Cork flag of the Norman invaders who sowed their seed inland and upland back home.

Hold him she would, Anna affirmed to herself, a calm visor of sheer bullheadedness swinging down across her face. Hold him she would, and raise him right, no matter what the bloody hell he looked like or how many of everything he'd got.

Anna had a million stories to tell her son already. The tales from home, the ones her papa and mama told, were the very bread in her mouth nowadays. Her boss, old Tesco down at the town library, made sure of that.

The dapper nonagenarian marked that specific hunger in her eyes when she took the broom from his arthritic hands in the lobby and pertly asked him if there was any work available.

"Mine own father built the first library here with his own collection," Tesco told her stiffly. "Uncle knew Jakob and Wilhelm Grimm, though not die Mutti . . ." though Anna never heard corroboration. Tesco was given to flamboyant embellishment, and for that, she loved him.

Town gossips only hissed that Tesco was "afflicted" and an "invert." But heaven knew that was the rumor lobbed at many, la vise Anglais—a handy cricket bat made of excrement and readily available.

But moreover, there was some trouble about Tesco and the local Ehrend iron-mining dynasty in the distant past, not that the Flemishman would ever speak of either thing or find them seemly. Any way around it, she had a different view of what made an abomination and what didn't. The view of caritas, empathy's open hand. A mother's love. Not only for fabulous inverts.

"'Twas God the Father made yeh so," Anna murmured now in Shamus's tiny, elfin ear. "An' His ways are not ours to understand. Mysterious His wonders to perform, an' all. Yer not . . . yer not *for* the priesthood, I don't think, though. 'Tis a teacher yeh'll be. Or a doctor. Or whatever in the wide world it's in your heart to be. Yer born an American, Shamus Joseph, so make the most of it with or without . . ."

*

This is the dream. I am Shamus Connelly now. Pauper. Not Taliesn Demarest, not Bastard Prince, no more. Into this time, I am born. Into this Great Depression thrown. Now I am the pale face, looking out of the front window in the reflection.

I've been outside once or twice, wrapped in a blanket, Papa's welding goggles hiding my light-starved eyes. I like the goggles. After a while, I reach for them and put them on myself.

I never cry. Papa thinks I'm a daemon. The feeling's mutual. Papa's out on the bad stuff again. I can tell. Blessed Mother will intercede on my behalf when God the Father gets home from the bar.

Papa gets something he calls "relief" from the mine company sometimes because he has trouble breathing and can't work as much. Now he makes his lung medicine in the big shiny copper thing out in the garage where he yells up, "Woman, shut it an' moynd yer business," quite a bit.

Part of me already asks, "Is all this why we came over then? Is this why we left home?" I know even then that Da' will turn ugly on me quickly. Unless I keep him laughing.

I know I'll forget all this when I get older and dumber. Like we all get older and dumber. But maybe I'll—

(we'll?)

—remember just enough.

Mrs. Burkhauser from Germantown likes me though. She watches me in the afternoons when Mama's shelving books at the library and Papa's working down at the mines, when he can get it, or out with his brothers and those other rough miners when he can't.

I see through Mrs. Burkhauser's mind when I take the time to look, when she holds me to her big bosom (where the six-pointed metal star is always worn under her shirt, never outside) and sings just so, in words I know aren't the same as Mama and Papa's mother tongue.

"Night by night . . .
The lone, singing star . . .
Sleep, oh sleep, put out the light . . .
Sleep, oh sleep, oh put out the light . . ."

Francezska Burkhauser cries when she sings that cradle song. I see into her mind. I see . . . I see . . . I see her language is something called Yiddische. She cries for someone I don't know. Someone who isn't here.

When she sings, I close my eyes and see her new, resigned tomb-world in this country, all alone just up the road where the railroad men all live in their ticky-tacky houses or long-frame hotels, which smell like low tide took a shit in the lobby, with nickel beers and communal bathrooms.

I see it all. I see it all, dancing far out across life in this crooked little town, my whole existence down to the inevitable crackle and boom. I know what I know.

"Most every year when the springtime comes,
And the birds begin to sing . . ."

Shamus's mum learned to play piano the first summer she was over from Cork. She played barrelhouse piano at the Orpheum Theater down on Main Street before they got the talkies in. That was good money for a while, one of eight or ten "odd jobs, bits and bobs" as Mum wryly referred to them, pin-money socked away in her plain navy-blue apron with the regularity of corn growing ears.

Anna still kept up with the piano, which kept Joe from hauling their old Hammond electrical organ out of the living room and down to the dump . . .

"The organ-grinder comes around
With a monkey on a string . . ."

At her feet, the pale boy in tie-on goggles clapped his poor gloved hands and cackled, singing along when he could keep a straight face. He knew what was coming. The song was an old chestnut you could hear anywhere on New York radio when they could get it on the big antenna. It was just the way Ma' got going when she got to the bridge that fairly slew him, each and every time no matter what . . .

Joe invariably sat in his armchair behind Anna and the boy, brooding. The boy was madly watching his mother's hands as though she were spinning straw into gold as she pounded the black keys, and even Joe himself hit the high notes on his old Hohner mouth organ, so their mutt Joker would attempt to howl along from the back porch, thumping his stringy two-tone tail on the bare gray boards.

"And the grinder and his monkey sit
Outside the grocery store . . ."

In the song, the boy is taken outside himself, outside his shadow box, jumping at everything, the startle response exaggerated threefold from the first time Joe ever cuffed him in the face . . .

(ah gods FFWD FFWD can't FWD can't FWD fast enough can't wake up . . . I am Taliesn Demarest, Heir of Shang 2, and I COMMAND you, Mandelbrot, stop showing me this . . .)

Four years old, reaching up too high for Daddy's work lantern, because it looked like Aladdin's lamp in the picture book but full of wet gray stones, smelling of raw burnt rock, and Joe had started in on the whiskey at four that afternoon, but he was the "bull of the woods around here! What I say goes, and anyway, the shit I got to put up with, raising a monster . . ."

"Joe, yeh just hit him in the head like he was one of your own mates . . ." And the schoolteacher Anna Connelly would neither call the sheriff nor put down the shotgun.

They forgot about it like they always did, forgave and forgot because heaven forfend the Church have to get involved or anyone with half an eye. Anna knew no one would, so she decided to build her ramparts higher, dig them in deeper and offer the rest to the Blessed Mother in prayer . . .

"The foolish things that monkey does,
They put me in a roar . . ."

As the bridge of the song came round, even Joe was powerless not to bellow a belly laugh, just like everyone else in the room, even (he would swear) Joker the dog,

"Now's the time the fun begins, AAAAhahahaahah . . .
How that monkey hops and grins, AAAAhahahaahah . . ."

The laughter and the song were always done too soon. But for the whole of his short, troubling life, Shamus never forgot the words.

THE GREAT HUNGER

Shamus J. Connelly, Grade 6
Brother Piper, English

COMPOSITION JOURNAL
RECOVERED FROM PERSONAL EFFECTS,
APPARENTLY UNGRADED. [CB]

November 10, 1940

Last night, I left my body and woke up in the dream again, in Nightmare Town, turning endlessly over fields lain bare by the stink of Man that killed all the critters worth saving. None to blame but us for the perversions that skitter and gambol through the underbrush out there on extra things like limbs, their eyeless faces acid-etched by railroad waste, never twice the same.

Lain bare, those moonlit blasted heaths, glowing an anxious color not out of space, just out of town a few miles. I thought I saw the sun come up just then.

In the walk of the waking dream, it was no sun at all but a tiny metal thing with a hundred thousand limbs like a sea urchin or an anemone. I opened my mouth and called it Mandelbrot. In the dream, it spoke in my mind, and it called me Tally. It called me friend.

I soared far overhead with Mandelbrot, drifting like a little kid's lost balloon. Listening to it talk and talk. Telling me things it wasn't for certain I'd remember when I woke unless I wrote them down. Always. Always. Wrote them. Down.

Mandelbrot was very stern but only about that. The rest of it, he was like a bloody little clockwork Peter Pan, the devil of him, and I was the better for flying around after with the sky in my hair and no pain in my hands at all. At all.

At all. It was the first time I'd dreamwalked for months, and it would have been kind of nice . . .

If not for the coldest, blackest fear that had ever tightened over my heart when I got close to the swamp outside of town.

Down in the mere there, I saw several pestiferous, slavering, misbred Yankee-gators grown to an enormous size, tearing down a house cat that got too close to the water. A poor tabby like my Wolfe. My dear Wolfe, to whom none would ever do such a bastard thing within the reach of my hands . . .

My hands. My hands were hanging me there in the air. Holding me still in the eye of their own particular lightning. Keeping me safe. Me own self. Keeping me safe.

Safe enough to see what I could see: something, something, something there was, avidly cheering on that bastard gator pit from the window of Ehrendhaus where the high-school kids go on dares and drink beers and sometimes come back a little . . . strange.

A little strange like something's in 'em. Something like bad worms. Bad worms that make them hungry for bad things.

Maybe it's just the codeine, but I dreamed. Lord, how I dreamed that night of something that loved a half-ruined wall. Something living—if such it could be termed—in the swamp just a few miles outside of town, sitting on a very large pile of very small bones by a ruined mansion that was new in the dim, dead days of the "Man with No Face," from all the old stories people tell in town . . .

Once, that thing actually walked on two legs as a man. I saw no face. My eyes could not perceive the horror of his face. Something that every part of me abhors. Something that is everything I am not.

Behind me, Mandelbrot was doing something stronger than my hands. Saying words I didn't understand to someone elsewhere, like over a wireless telegraph. Trying not to talk too loudly. Part of me had the spare half second to wonder why.

I could hear the other thing, the thing living in the swamp. The thing that lived partly in, and through, the house in the swamp, cackling with glee as it felt my clueless, disembodied soul being drawn to it like a soap chip headed for a bathtub drain.

That bad wind, that wendigo, as the Lenape called the Man with No Face in these woods, began reeling me in the moment my all-unknowing head hit the pillow. I woke, I walked. I ran from it, ran and ran with my hands screaming and my mouth screaming me awake.

I always run and lose the magic of the dreamwalk until the next time I can relax enough to do it again. Around my house, that's not any too often.

Dreams such as those, dope dreams or no, are more than most people in my age can handle, only a little peephole into the nothing that we fight every day by living. There isn't always an accurate record of anything in the rocks or on the walls or anywhere.

Sometimes disaster doesn't wait up for someone to take pictures of it. Real history just *happens*. And it's like Time and Space themselves link hands, standing still just long enough for you to click the shutter on your battered old camera.

In that moment of grace, you can see how much of it was *deliberate*: kettledrums of marching feet, violins of dying screams, cymbals of battlefield smoke, and the kilns of burning dead, all conducted by one hand.

Different years. But the face is always the same. From the dreams. Typhon Demarest's jaundiced junkie face mutated out of all countenance by a future I cannot permit myself to understand.

Typhon's dehumanizing, dehumanized face. Every broken mind and world war all shot to pieces when that beast shows so easily that after a while the same old song starts to skip on the Victrola from the scratch, calling back a million nightmares that elders laughed away . . .

But we've always had a choice, I realize now as I sit here in class goofing off with my heart breaking in the effort of explaining not necessarily my means of arriving here—this odd cough syrup Ma' gives me for my asthma and the bronchitis, which just sets me OFF—but what I *found* . . .

If they, Da' and some of the brothers and the whole kit and caboodle of them, would so damn me for having probed the darkness of the human intellect without bothering to even care or grasp what I found there, then let me say I shall remain for all time damned, damned, damned, and damn proud to be so.

Da' hung all my idols on trees with ten-penny nails. With those horrible memories comes the unspoken promise now to never be gentle with anyone's false idols if they look a thing like Da', the kind who wire up the worshipper to blindly follow someone else off the cliff.

Da' and his ilk hate Pinkertons. Perhaps I'll go be a Pinkerton guard then, or even a private eye if they'd hire a cripple. God A'mighty, what a dream that would be. Ma' says I can do anything and to tell her when I've found that thing.

I just might, journal. I just might tonight. But the adversary I see in those dreams, journal, is more than me and my stupid hands.

How many times must we see innocence stolen, anything worthwhile for its own sake torn out and butchered in the most immediate, senseless manner possible? We won't let the little ones sleep with a light on, and then we wonder why their beds are empty in the morning.

Oh yes. Even around here. I listen at the barbershop, where Mister Connors always gives me a lolly or a bit of horehound candy, though I'm nearly thirteen.

I hear the old men in Connors' Barbershop, talking about the Troubles long ago and the debased Church of Starry Wisdom up in the hills, near Bull's Crick and Blackbird Pie and all those little bumps in the road without a name where folk don't go. All the things they shut up about when little pitchers with great big Mickey Finn ears such as mine draw near to hand.

The babbies who never came back. All the tiny little headstones with not much on them but tears and tears and tears. The ones not quite babbies found . . . in bits in the cricks, or sometimes wandering and raving and silver-eyed, with things done to them no one ought to have done. And worse.

They don't know I still hear: there, or in the quiet kitchens on the restaurant side of the American Hotel where Crazy Hazel the cook still talks of all she can in tiny whispers, mumbling to herself as she works in the back, well away from the customers, about the pieces of her babby that were all he left her, about *he* in the first place, and what *his* existence might mean . . .

Blaming gets us nowhere. We have to start, journal, by finding *all* the clues. Not just the ones that fit what we think—*all* of them. Only then may we begin to form a testable hypothesis, before we even *think* about a theory. Only then, as Sir Arthur Conan Doyle's stories showed me, may we even *think* of removing the impossible.

My name is Shamus Connelly, and if Edgar Allan Poe can change what it means to be a detective, then so the bloody hell can I. Good night, journal. Always so much more to say.

OLD LADY TWOHEAD

Nov. 20, 1940

Must write in this again. Will help. Will help now

.

In the morning, we wash our hands. Da' shows me every time with the pumice soap to get all the little ins and outs and bits that I forget. This morning, he wasn't there to do that. And I was glad. God help me, Jesus, Mary, and Joseph, but I was glad.

We don't talk about my hands in this house, you see. We make allowances. We go to Confession. We come down twice as hard on him and ourselves and each other as we ever would otherwise, but do we make note of it in daylight?

No. We make moonshine. We make trips to the pharmacy. We make believe . . .

In the morning, we wash our hands. Da's hands are always black, even now. He says the pumice never gets the coal dust all the way off. But he also says that when you wash your hands, the water washes away your sins. I don't know if he means what he thinks he means . . .

I send the bad away into the water like I knew how to do since I was born. I send away all the poison from town, from home, from everywhere, back into the poison water.

And my hands start to . . . do something when I do, my poor umbrella hands that feel all numb and half-there. I learn to scry in the sink like a bloody pagan witch, to scry in the water and let the fingers zap and spark when the bad goes away and I can feel . . .

I scry with my little eye why Da' hasn't come home today.

I scry the big, perpetually coal-dusty, perpetually blood-blistered hands that played the harmonica and beat blue stripes on my ass, that wrapped presents and sewed wounds, built houses and bent elbows and . . .

I scry one of those hands, protruding from a smoking black column of rubble, far under the earth where no regular human person could get down to and see.

I scry what put them there: the hideous blue flare of methane from far below and the crump of blast-wave that gave them no time to run, run, RUN from the shelf of rock that came down atop them, the high, gurgly screams of the dead and the dying.

I scry this in the bathroom at school. Even before Mr. Myelnik from the mine office comes and pulls me from study hall.

Every night, I used to pray to God the Father Almighty that I didn't have to go work in the mines with Da' when I turned twelve or so. That day has barely passed. The dream-voice in the back of my mind—who calls himself Taliesn like the singer in the old tales, Tally Demarest with the fine old name—tells me that my path lies over the hills and far away, just an afternoon's drive by car, in the city that doesn't sleep.

But he's pretty sure it dreams. That's good. I dream too. I dream about New York a lot.

A lot. Sometimes I wake up in the graveyard at the end of my block, wrapped in a blanket and not much else. Sometimes my nose is bleeding. But I never hit my head. Sometimes the blood looks like mercury. Sometimes it isn't really there.

I don't tell Ma about that. She'd have a bird if she knew I was out of the house. I try to tell her I can clean my teeth and comb my hair and do everything a "real boy" can, but I'll always and ever be her little Flipper Baby, as the high-school kids sometimes call me.

Flipper Baby or sometimes Flipper or Flip for brevity, Scorpion Boy and Ducky and that horrid chant from the old movie I thought was wonderful, though these townie bastards can turn even that into a mockery, "ONE OF US . . . ONE OF US . . . GOOBLE, GOBBLE, WE ACCEPT YOU, WE ACCEPT YOU," that they keep up at me for blocks down around Eighteenth Street until the black kids show up and beat their Kraut asses back to their own neighborhood.

God bless those black boys. I've no truck with them. None of us go to the same school. Who knows anybody? They can fight.

The black kids never bother me in that part of town. They don't talk to me, but they let me walk through.

I know why. There's a Voodoo lady I met, a beautiful old Voodoo lady with hair like snakes done up on the top of her head in a big, braided crown.

Her real name's Delphine. Delphine Saint-Ange. Says it on her mail slot. She's old, older than Grandma Dot, but I can see what she looked like when she was young.

She has the kindest eyes, and she was out on her porch on Circle Avenue—the one that just makes a turnout a block away from where it starts—one day when I passed through. Hers is the big, amber-colored house with the screened porch, in the middle of the three.

First time I met Mrs. Saint-Ange, she smelled like a spice rack to me, if a spice rack could move around and make tea and smoke cigars. She came out and gave me a gingersnap, right out of the oven, and fussed over my hands in a language I didn't quite understand. Sounded like French, but only half. The other half was something I never heard before, anywhere, ever.

"My name's Shamus, missus. Shamus Connelly," I said when she asked. "What's yours?"

That got a gold-toothed grin, and the scary feeling started to leave the porch. "You call me Ol' Lady Twohead, bwai." She saw the look. "No, it don't work literal. It is a title of respect. I been around a long time." She shook herself. "Do you like a gingersnap, boy detective? Milk, too, today. Dairyman come Monday, and Mama Twohead still bakin'."

Missus Saint-Ange was looking into my soul, and it made me step back. Because I could see into hers.

Someone else lived in this old shaman-woman's dreams. Two someones. Joined at the hip. Joined at the guts and black as her, black as coal. Two black angels. Twins. Something like conjoined twins.

I go see Mama Twohead sometimes when I'm sad. She's not well, but safe. Safe. Every time I can sneak up there, I do. Because one day, I won't be able to.

Every morning, I wash my hands, plunge them in the basin up to the wrists, and try to ask God to show me what I need to know. Sometimes, He answers. Most of the time, though, He only tells me that I already know it . . .

Most of the time, I make flip-books in class when I should be studying or paying attention. Most of the time, Mum and I raise the monarch butterflies in the fall, bring them here in the house to the screen cage we built, and watch them spin their chrysalides, smell the smell of transubstantiation, the small gold seam that is the last stitch sealing up the teal shell . . .

"Is it all right I'm glad Da's dead?" I asked later. After the thing happened. The terrible thing. The cave-in. Mama Twohead's eyes were always distant.

"God understand," was always her only comment. "God nah judge you for that. Not nah good boy like you." And she couldn't have been more serious if all three of her lives depended upon it.

But Da' never really left, living on in component parts. There was Uncle Bud who always took him fishing and asked after his Ma' and showed him how to cut four-by-sixes and square up a new porch rail. Uncle Bud who taught him the first chamber of his own Snuffy Smith-like logic that, "Yeh don't go fishin' to catch no fish, boyo. Fishing is church with no roof."

There was Pap-Pap, bless his heart, who always found a way to get down off the hill and teach Shamus the finer points of electronics and plumbing and all the weird bits and bobs of things the Connellys picked up simply because learning to fix something was cheaper than spending money they didn't have to feed the planned obsolescence monkey, one of Pap-Pap's very favorite soapboxes . . .

"Some folks go out and buy a new one,'" Michael Connelly rounded on the world, looking up into the sweet gray smoke of his pipe in the incandescent trouble light above the basement workbench. "Some folk can't even think of sooch a thing, lad. Yeh got to make do and, more importantly, make work. Oh, there it goes."

At his feet, Shamus hid a smile. The tip of one webbed finger wove the air in concert with the antenna on the radio, and the ball game came back on. "OH NO, FOLKS, JOLTIN' JOE GOT ALLA THAT ONE . . . TRIIIPLE PLAAAY!!! IT'S A RED-LETTER DAY HERE AT YANKEE STADIUM—"

"That's done it," Pap-Pap nodded, only seeing the boy's metal glove thoughtfully raised up like an aerial. "That was smart there. Now hush, lad, and hold your hand still. The Yanks are goon'ta take this'n right home to the cleaners . . ."

Shamus Connelly sat and listened to the ball game at the time, but of many a lightning storm that night, he dreamed, he dreamed, he dreamed . . .

ADJUSTING THE AMPERAGE

Shamus never forgot the first time he ever wound up bright red, stripped to the waist, and clamped down to Dr. Drebel's newest toy. "Now, Shamus, this is a new-fangled machine. May help you get some more motion in some of the . . . some of the fingers. I will apply one electrode to either hand and turn the juice up verrrrrrry slowly, and you just tell me how much you can . . ."

Then miracle and medical science met in the middle and exploded in midair.

"*A, B, C, D, E, F, G* . . . don't shoosh me, Doc. Sometimes it helps if I sing a simple song when this happens at home, makes it—oh! That smarts. *H* . . . *I* . . . *J* . . . *K* . . . don't come any closer. Pap-Pap says if you were to touch me, your head would shrink an' turn black, says he saw this once in England. Mr. Dickens even wrote of it—*oh god oh Doc please don't please . . . don't . . . touch me, or I think . . . I think you'll die.*"

"How is this possible? My boy, my boy, remain still! I'll be damned if you aren't being . . . struck by . . . something. Let the . . . the 'electric fluid,' let it crawl down from your hands to the . . . to the ground, that is all it seeks! Let it . . .

"*L* . . . *M, N, O* . . . *P—oh my Jaisus, Mary, n' Joseph and all the Saints preserve us that just about fookin KIIIIILLS—*"

At length, the doctor found his voice. "My God. I have a hole in my fine linoleum floor and Anna Connelly's son with second-degree burns on his palms. My boy—no, shut that door. Surely they all must have heard out in the waiting room. My boy, I am going to have a medicinal shot for my nerves just now. Then we are going to bandage you. And we will speak of this to no one, yes?"

Shamus beamed. "Oh aye, Da' already whaled the tar out of me for it once. Thought I was playin' wi' matches. Heh. I let him have that, erm . . . side of things, yeh see. It . . . would do him less harm. I did love the old knockabout. I know he couldn't help bein' completely mental. We all are . . . sorry, I'm still trembling. Would you look . . . at this . . . will it . . . will it go down, do you suppose?"

Doctor Drebel was immediately adamant. "Yes, yes, with a bandage and a few good washings with clean water and salt. Maybe carbolic—oh, put the face away, not much, and highly diluted. There's a good lad. No one hears of this. They would lock us both away. "

"Right. And Ma' don't hear any more than she must? Please? Doctor?" His lower lip trembled, and he looked like a real boy again. "Sir?"

"Leave that to me. Heh. What a caution you are, young Shamus. I was just saying to my nurse, 'It's a wonderful age we're living in in some respects. Think how our children get interested in things we never dreamed of when we were growing up.'"

There was a sad look in his eyes, a wistful one. "I will help you, my boy. I always knew there was something special about you. Good heavens. Does anyone else know about this?"

"I . . . Mama Twohead—old Mrs. Saint-Ange on Eighteenth Street I told yeh of."

"Delphine." The doctor's eyes grew warm. "Delphine who brings me gingerbread cookies like we had back home. I put a cast on her arm when she broke it baling hay at her brothers'. Now cookies, on the day it was done, and my birthday. Yes. Anyone else?"

Shamus exhaled deeply. "Chang Lo, a mate of mine from school. He found out quite by accident. His Papa—his Papa Tien—he says . . . he can help me, a little, but I haven't been down yet. He was a doc too where he come from, an' he says he knew a man wi' the same affliction—"

This was news. The doctor had to sit down a bit. It had been several geological minutes since his last glass of plum wine down at Tien's spot.

"Ho! Ho! Ha! The old dragon himself wants to snap you up! Ha! Well, like most of the herbs he pushes, it couldn't do any real harm. Anyway, most importantly, black herbalists like Delphine, and Chinese sages like old Tien-Sifu, they know how to respect someone's privacy, even if they are exceptional like you. More than I can say for half the white people in this town, and more's the pity . . ."

Soon enough, the mess was all swept away. Long after the boy left, the doctor took a second shot to calm his nerves, still wondering what that . . . other kind of doctor might take it into his odd head to do.

"Not my circus," Dr. Drebel quoted a carny whose lacerated arm he'd doused in carbolic and bandaged, "not my monkeys."

But in the deepest chambers of his clinical mind, he was less than sure.

In Brother Domenick's Applied Sciences class the next morning, in the big, clangy white shop-space of Science Hall, Shamus Connelly heard nothing but the wind's weird melody he'd first known when he stood at the kitchen window on a foggy morning gazing upon the gray woods and asked Ma' what the magic roaring meant, blowing across the valley.

The wind carried a storm with it today, darkening the graveyard everywhere they could see from the window. Occasionally, there was a faraway snap of lightning. It was making Shamus's hands hurt already, but he knew it would bypass them. Because they *just* hurt.

He glanced over at Cricket Bennigan and saw the girl biting a pencil point with her absolutely adorable overbite he didn't know if she knew was adorable. The hair falling to her neck was fine and yellow like corn silk. Early sunlight streamed through the window and fell upon the floor in the aisle between them, making an irregular pattern.

"When I was little," Cricket whispered, giggling, "I scared my mom half to death. There was a thunderstorm, and I was standing up in my crib, laughing. She said I tried to open up the window and play with the lightning . . ."

"QUIET," Brother Dom said without looking, but it was a moot point. Shamus turned beet-red when she spoke to him, opening his mouth and trying to make sounds come out. Cricket's eyes flicked back down to her work as Brother Dom's panopticon gaze swung over them. Shamus filled in the form at the top of the tablet, writing "Apr.03" after *Date*.

Shamus found it difficult to concentrate. The morning was filled with distractions. The soft spring wind, sweeping from the newly cultivated fields outside town, brought a warm breath of soil through the open door. Out in the schoolyard, a sea of lilies had begun to poke out their fey white heads in spots where they'd soon enough be mown down.

Flutterings of pigeons came from up in the belfry, and he recalled again his first year of school, remembering the dream world in distant spheres, kneeling among a long equation in which the solution was never satisfactory, there being no answer book for reference, no process for checking . . .

Then just like that, the waking Dreamwalk took Anna Connelly's only son Shamus, and he was asleep in class, up, up, and out of the old rooming house that Our Lady of the Alleghenies Secondary School had been, all the teratological dream-imprints of every incarnation of the building whacking together badly, looking kind of like a filthy public bog like the one way south in Altoona at the bus station.

Shamus slithered down to the purest electric fluid that was himself, got up and out through the water in one of the old copper pipes, and crackled swiftly down the telephone wire outside the window.

He was conscious only of his sudden unbearable lightness, the wire brighter than day, and the sense of forward motion whistling past his ears. He had no heartbeat now as he understood such a thing in these kinds of dreams, but the pulse that was himself felt like an incessant bullfrog, croaking and croaking in his chest as he shot out into the cold Monongahela River, great mirror recording the minutes of town.

Stark and solid and victorious, the dream-lightning faded from him like some other kind of blood in shorter supply and became a haunting memory that burned and ached.

It occurred to Shamus that happiness was a method of travel, not necessarily a destination. There was a thirst that drank and drank but knew no final quenching. There was an elusive dream that slipped away, leaving always the mountains, the gloomy mountains and people in that literary and topographical vacuum south of the Poconos and the Catskills and the Hamptons, just slightly north of hell . . .

I never forgot the first time I drew down the lightning awake. My hand was wet. The plate on the outlet was almost half out of the wall. It was dark. At home.

I pissed myself when the arcing snakes bit me, the twin fangs of POS NEG twining from the plug. But my hand and arm . . . stayed blue.

This wasn't at the doctor's office. I really could learn to do things with this, myself. I remembered the gloomy, paste-smelling library at Our Lady, shuffling my military brogans with their killing gloss across the gray institutional carpet and zapping Cricket Bennigan in the back of the neck with the tip of one index finger.

I remember feeling the recoil of the shock in the fillings of my teeth much worse than Cricket's involuntary sock in the jaw with one tiny fist, and the noise she made. I remember laughing.

Sister Ninian kicked the shit out of me for that, and I was howling laughter the whole time. Sister swore I had a joy buzzer, and I threw it away before she got there, you see. To the school principal, Attilla the Nun herself, Sister swore this thing. So much for her. Miserable old beast.

I thought I understood my ability then. But there was much more to come. Like the day I met the writer . . .

Shamus bumped into the man, knocking the copy of *Weird Tales* out of his hand, face up. They both bent to pick it up and nearly knocked heads.

The stranger was too tall for his own good, Pap-Pap would have said, with patent-leather hair slicked back from a high forehead, a strange jaw, and a fishy aspect to his visage. His gray suit was as proper as a banker's yet looked like it had been slept in on a train or a bus.

The stranger picked up the magazine, almost handed it to him, and then visibly startled at the sight of Shamus's hands. "You poor child." His Rhode Island patois was clipped, almost English. "Do they give you much pain?"

Shamus seesawed one hand, watching the way the dark eyes followed its tiniest motion. "A bit. Not like you'd think though. Had 'em all my life."

The man permitted himself a small chuckle. "Well, you truly have wonderful taste in literature. If we might duck into Mr. Lusardi's excellent drugstore and find pen and ink, I would be most happy to inscribe—"

Shamus's eyes glowed. He wasn't really listening. "You know these kinds of stories? I thought only kids—"

The New Englander winced, hissed, and placed an avuncular hand on Shamus's shoulder, pointing to the second line of type on the cover. "They are the very bread in my mouth."

At the dazed look of slow comprehension, the stranger's eyes narrowed, and he began to smile. Then belly laugh. "Do I know them?" he asks. "They are my comrades. A lot of them write me letters. They call me Uncle." He looked again, happily, at the byline.

The second line of type, the second story in the magazine, under a new one by Clark Ashton Smith, read, "The Strange Case of Charles Dexter Ward, by Howard Phillips Lovecraft."

"Wow." Shamus shook his hand. Howard shuddered, shook it back, and involuntarily wiped his own hand on his gray trousers. (The boy used the same hand to hide his smile.)

"A real-live scientifiction writer in Powersburg. Never knew what one looked like. Tell us this"—he grinned more broadly—"is there truly such a book as the *Necronomicon*?" Shamus's look betrayed him. "That is . . . um, er . . . anyplace? Ever? Was it?"

Howard let Shamus lead him down the crumbled flagstone walk in the direction of Sal's drugstore. He was warming up to the discussion. "Not a word, my boy, not a word. The Mad Ay-rab whom canon tells us penned that foul, vile volume was none other than mine own nom-de-plume when I was first dallying with the written word and wearing short pants."

Now it was Shamus's turn to belly laugh. "Aw, what a joke. Not a bad one, either. You had me goin', you did. I suppose . . ." His smile wanted to cover the horizon. "I suppose that's kinda the whole point of why you do what you do, yeah?"

He was excited by this. It felt like a lovely thing to know. But Lovecraft looked like he just bit through a horseapple. His eyes went all scowly, and his mouth twitched, just to the left.

"What is concealed, or revealed, in the poor purple prose of my hobby, is a matter on which you and I could get through many stamps and ideas. You're a good boy, Mr. Connelly." His eyes were still somewhere else, and strange. "But there are *books* . . ."

Something about this was difficult for him. Shamus couldn't quite get a read. Howard's pale, scholarly brow furrowed and wrinkled and reddened at the wrinkles, becoming something that looked like it belonged in a jar at the carny. Clearly, he loved to pontificate when he had an audience.

"There are books, master Shamus, books and books which may have outlasted the crusades, the terrible conflagrations at Tripoli and Alexandria. Ur and Ubar and mighty Kush and Meroe, and"—here he named a city Shamus couldn't even think, let alone spell—"and elsewhere, all have yielded treasures greater and more terrible than our poor science today could credit. Fragments of such books have traveled to many . . . a strange corner of the world."

Howard looked him in the eyes, then saw that Shamus was listening and continued. "I believe that one of them is here. In the ruins of the ironmaster's house, it is said, stolen from a debased Mennonite who used it to call up all manner of unholiness before something got into him and killed him dead. Old Sollenheim was exiled because of that book. They said it 'exercised an unhealthy hold.' That it was worldly, of the English, forbidden . . . but also forbidden by the English! The debased cult that sprang up around its use is called Starry Wisdom. Do you know of it?"

Shamus was uncertain. "You don't . . . you couldn't mean the Red Caps? Those boggarts out in the hills that my da' says . . . said . . . used to steal the coal?"

Howard nodded. "No matter. I do go on. The book was translated by Nostradamus in the Middle Ages, but the actual text is much, much older. Nostradamus merely redacted it and veiled the story entire in his own little four-line poems."

Shamus's eyes were full of stars. "Gosh, Mister Lovecraft, that's the best story I ever heard anyone make up off the cuff in my . . . ever! My ma' says I'm going to be a private eye like Philip Marlowe when I grow up, so maybe I can help you look for that book. Me and my best mate, we could go out to the swamp and . . ."

But he stopped. Howard stood there on the sidewalk, wobbling slightly, with a look of wild and continuous grief burning down those eyes that were far too dark for purported Mayflower blood.

"That way lies madness," he told Shamus. "Though I am in but ill health myself, never in my life upon this earth would I charge such a clearly beloved mother's son"—Shamus grimaced—"with the awful task that awaits me. I pour out my soul to the first poor crippled child I see. I am truly in ruins. I may well be picked up off the street and thrown in irons for simply opening my big mouth. I must be losing my mind. I . . . I shouldn't have undertaken this . . . I am lost . . ."

Shamus was lost himself. His lower lip trembled. He really just wanted a soda and didn't understand all this weird grown-up insanity coming out of such a great writer in the flesh. He waited, letting the man come back into his senses. When Howard did, emotion marched across his granite face in neon letters nine miles wide.

"I must take you into my confidence, for no part of anything I just said was made up. It's not a story at all, my boy, and the longer I remain in this town, the more I only wish it were. I may escape with my sanity . . ."

Their visit to the drugstore was brief, and not much more was said. He'd upset him, Shamus saw, and kept the signed copy of *Weird Tales* after he paid for their two bottles of Moxie with part of his allowance from Mum.

Lovecraft patted him on the head, left his address, and told Shamus to write to him. But he never answered one letter, and after their meeting, his stories took a grim turn, one that lasted for quite a while. *Like he'd been scared quite badly . . .*

"Connelly, you fuckin' retard, get off the ball field with your little Woolworth catcher's mitt before I knock you upside the—"

That was about all I heard. I made what fist I could with my right hand and poleaxed Dave Johnson in the jaw with my big wrist-glove still on. Doctor Drebel would have shot me for a stranger, but he wasn't out there to help either.

The other members of the baseball team were gone, like gangsters from the scene of a hit. The play yard was full of wind and words.

Something left me when I pasted him though. I felt it spark the metal in my gloves, the five big metal fingers and one metal thumb Doc Drebel made for me to work with all the extra fingers I got inside of them.

I felt Dave bite through his tongue. I heard him scream, and when he pissed his pants, it steamed a bit.

It steamed. They all saw. All of them saw, but none of them said anything to Sister Ninian or anyone.

I think they're scared of me now. They still don't talk to me, but something else is wrong . . .

Something else was wrong. I knelt, pulling open Dave's eyes. They should have had one TILT sign each like in the cartoons. The irises were flat Woolworth-mannequin rings. There was foam at his mouth, he . . .

"Shamus," Sister Beverley the Principal, Attilla the Nun herself, said above and behind me, looming like an H. Rider Haggard idol, "you defended yourself. You'll go to Confession, but you tell Father to come see me if he has any questions. David has epilepsy. What you are seeing is called a seizure. That means that his brain just had a thunderstorm. You wait. Watch, we get him on his side until the nurse comes. She'll have a block of wood to put in his mouth. We were told of this . . ."

So many things didn't make sense in life. I never got a school picture, and they said it was because the cameras went funny when I was about, and no one was to ever talk of it. I could only ever listen to the radio at night, and even then, I could barely hear the dialogue. Except at Pap's.

Because there was the big antenna . . . and also a grand big ground-wire, going under the workbench on staples. Because of the lightning storms. I figured that part out myself.

No one wanted to talk about any of that, in school or at home. No one in my family talked about anything that mattered, except Ma', and she only did when no one else was around . . .

"A little guilt is a good thing. Keeps you in line. But in the name of God, son, you can't blame yourself for this because"—Sister's whiskery, hooded-eyed face leaned in close to his, her breath like blueberries on oatmeal—"it just don't add up!"

In her eyes, the pale red-haired boy in his smoked glasses saw himself reflected back, a flame of fear with the black cloth liners behind the gloves pulled way up into his cuffs. He still hadn't gotten over being in regular classes with regular children, even three years in—there was no school for crippled children anywhere near Powersburg. The Peterson twins both had Down syndrome, poor girls, though smart enough; Jimmy Chipman was stone blind from birth. Many more of their students were likewise.

When she was a girl in the farm country around Glastonbury, Sister Beverly, the former Shandeen Cruikshank, once watched her father tote home a sack of chickens from the manufactory farm up the road.

The manufactory chickens all stayed in the coop, in the dark and moved into the light only in a defensive circle at first until they saw there was no threat from the rest of the flock, only curiosity. So far, that entirely described Shamus's secondary education.

"I'm giving you enough demerits to choke a grown goat for knocking someone down with those gloves on. This is the third time I've told you, Connelly. They are not defensive weapons. If you were an adult, you could be tried for some very serious charges. You get down on your knees and thank God you're a cripple, or you'd be in a world of hurt."

When she saw by his face that he was properly chastened, she let up. "On the other hand, Dave would have had that seizure somewhere, somehow. You may have just acted as God's instrument. Food for thought, Connelly. We'll make an Aquinas out of you yet if you'd just slow down and study more."

When he left, he looked like a punch-drunk boxer. That was good, and noted. He was paying attention. She wondered what he was always writing . . .

(unlabeled Fragment—CB)

Early dawn, and already the push-cart vendors along the Pike Road that hadn't been frightened to death by the debased hillfolk, or eaten, were making their defeatist rounds to sell what they could in the dawn light.

Still mounted, the pale rider moved through them under the high walls of the dirty old town. If any approached him, he gave them a glare and put the touch on them. This turned them pale and polite and made their hair stand on end.

"Keep quiet. Don't move. Life may still be sweet for you," Lord Gwai said, as his blade itched to circumnavigate the rival warlord's throat.

"You killed my father—" Yee On began, but his tongue stilled at the touch of cold steel.

"He was going to kill me first, and by surprise. Yet I would not have taken his life. Now I will take your own—"

Shamus put down his pen, pretending he'd just been staring off into space, as Brother Dom began showing them rudimentary plans for the suspension bridge they'd be grouping up to build as a science project.

The morning was thick with a heavy blue fog. Outside the window where he always spent so much time looking over the tops of the houses and tombstones and mausoleums, the line where earth met sky had never seemed as close as it did that year despite the best efforts of many.

The boy felt like he could run until he reached the horizon. The whole world was his to get up to monkeyshines with, his and his best friend's: good, quiet Lo with his fresh perspective on everything, his twinkling eyes that never mocked, and the gazillion wonderful things he knew how to do like make kites and catch crickets and build a fish pole from scratch.

And the Magic. The Magic his Zufu, his pap, brought with him from a place called Fo Shan. The magic of the wooden man, like the dummy Chang Tien had in his apartment. The magic of "Kung-fu."

Chang Lo's life was far from perfect, and he talked a lot about that. But no bully at school could get near him. "Teach me," Shamus always begged, later. Lo was resolute. "No. But he might. If you act grown-up about it and don't beg him . . ."

Now Shamus's thoughts rambled in haunting verses in the sunlight, still waking up. Out past the window and the graveyard, just south of Brickyard Hill, a dwarf peach tree in full bloom was shedding its blossoms like rain.

Just beyond it, three telegraph riggers were running a section of green glass wire and ornate crossbeams around and to the side to avoid the tree. In one flat moment, Shamus saw electricity lick from the wire and touch one of them, a stocky little red-haired fellow who greatly resembled his own cousin Kirk.

Half-horrified, Shamus watched the man fall, helpless. His comrades dropped down to him like spiders. His hair was smoking. Shamus couldn't see any closer. He bit his tongue, and—

"CONNELLY," Brother Dom thundered over his blueprint scrolls from the front of the room, voice thudding like a washtub bass.

"H-heard, Brother. Not in good voice today. I s-said, yes, I don't mind being in Group B. M-Mum can donate a good many Popsicle sticks as well."

"Hhmph," The Franciscan processed this. "Good form, Connelly. See me after class. I'll write down for your dear mother *about* how many we'll need. She's letting our fourth graders have a few field days at the library during her volunteer hours for a whole morning, bless her sainted heart . . ."

"Oh, aye," he smirked. "Story hour. You should hear the ones at home. She's got more than anybody."

The brother permitted himself the smallest of smiles. "Of that, I have no doubt. Moving on . . ."

Shamus's own heart was pounding in his chest, and his hands felt like the very agonies of Christ. A line of poetry from English class echoed along in his ears: *the lightning flies not swifter than the fall, nor thunder louder than the ruin'd wall.*

Outside and far too close, the little red-headed fellow appeared to be okay after he got up and shook it off and then let his mates talk to him a little and light him a cigarette. Shamus wondered if telephone and light repairmen were struck by lightning more frequently than the average Joe.

He made a mental note to ask Pap-Pap, his ma's da', about that. Pap-Pap retired as a lineman from Callaight County with a pension. Though he got crankier the worse his eyesight got, if you caught him right, he'd show you every weird little invention he ever made for his own use or anyone else's.

And the last time he was over, Pap-Pap passed on his prized black felt snap-brim hat to Shamus's wondering hands. "Oh, aye, heh. Lookitim, Anna. He found that old one I never wear. Give's a look at youse, Shamus Joseph. If the hat's a good fit, yeh can surely take it home. Yer grandmother says it stinks of Cutty Pipe. Oh, to be sure, yer head's as big as mine, for yer half a foot taller, even at your age . . ."

From the end of his life backward, Shamus would remember the day Pap-Pap gave him the gray Fedora with the thin black band. The one his mum said made him look like a private eye, and Lo said it made him look like a two-bit hood in some gangster flick about Al Capone.

Pap-Pap, who said his da' never should have sired children so soon. Pap-Pap, who he once saw cuff Shamus's own father. They'd been in the dooryard, two banty roosters puffing up about money and scratching in the dirt. Da' took the birdbath down with him when he went, and Shamus bit a hole in his cheek, so he wouldn't laugh out loud.

His ma' said such things weren't nice, "No matter how much the sotty git has it comin' to him, we must turn the other cheek and thus make *him* look the fool, yeh remember. When yeh love yer enemies, it heaps coals of fire down on their heads. Or I'll heap fire across your backside, yeh. Oh, now yeh've got me laughin', yeh caution. All right, just keep it to yerself in front of the grownups, but ain't he funnier than the very village eejit when he wants to be."

Shamus would never forget the day either, when he scuffed his feet on the carpet upstairs in Pap-Pap's house, making unintended static electricity in the darkness, crinkling one, just one, of the long red hairs on the second knuckle of his ring finger, running up his body like the ghost of a flea, making the muscles in his neck do things he couldn't understand, filling his poor eyes with light behind the smoked lenses.

Pap-Pap was an electrician. After he retired, he opened up that little shop of his in the basement of their old house on Grant Street, the house he and his brothers built from the scooped stone up.

Pap-Pap died of a heart attack when Shamus was sixteen. He kept the Fedora until the end.

Pap-Pap died of silence, a gray silence that slapped him down, a whistly, wintry silence that curled up around the sides of the big house he and his brothers dug into the side of the hill while his da' was still a surly lout bursting his spots.

When Pap-Pap died, Shamus got a little strange for a while. Lo came over to the house and tried to get things moving again. He suggested they play detective.

Shamus said some scary things about his dreams that didn't quite make any sense. Lo just gave him his head, as he was mourning a venerable ancestor. But between the two of them, somehow a destination took shape.

Shamus said something about their particular game of Sherlock Holmes that day being for HP Lovecraft, though "on our own hook, yeh see. Mister Lovecraft don't know we're goin' to get the big, weird book we were both dreamin' about. The . . . what'd you call it, Bible of Giants?"

Lo looked miffed. "Titans. The words were in Mandarin. Titans are worse than giants."

Shamus processed this and shrugged. " Maybe he'll write a story about it for *Weird Tales*."

Lo looked at him very sadly. "HP Lovecraft died about two years ago. It was in *Weird Tales*. They said no more Kathullahu stories. Or however you say it, smarty-eyes. I remember."

Shamus processed this. "All the more reason to go an' look then."

Lo threw up his hands. Sometimes there was just no talking your best friend out of anything.

BACK IN THE SHAFT

The first thing Lo and Shamus ran past was the old slag mill. Its marble troughs stretched away behind it for what looked like miles out back, with little hands bobbing in the green goop way way out in it. Or so Lo said. Shamus could not confirm this.

Lightning struck the ground violently at regular intervals, especially around the long ropes of dead animals strung out on nooses along certain backroad driveways every half mile or so to keep the redcaps out. Onward they sped at the time, but later they remembered how fast they ran to avoid what they might or might not have seen.

How fast both of them *knew* to run when they were "back in the Shaft" to avoid getting the shit knocked out of them: Shamus for being "crippled" and a "retard" and, worst, a "Catholic," and Lo for being a "Chink-Chink-China-Boy," and uglier things. It was simply that neither boy truly knew how fast they *could* run, or from what, or from what they thought they saw that yelled at them behind the others, who were yelling worse things that all blended into goblin glossolalia, after a while, in voices that could barely form sentences, the whole way down that little stretch of Sticktown Road to Heaven Hill Road, running like stump-jumpers, running for their lives . . .

Ehrendhaus. They remembered. The ruins of Ehrendhaus sat out in the middle of the woods like someone left it there, let it rot there and grow there on the long promontory that stretched into the swamp for half a mile.

They heard laughter coming from the property two miles away, but when they arrived at the ruined mansion, now a disturbing exploded diagram of what was, no one was there to greet them. Only rooms, and parts of rooms, old toys in the attic stomped down against the walls. Only the sense of a big hole.

"What's that smell?"

Silence stretched long between them.

"My good friend, that smell is death. Death for a long, long time. Like back home in Fo Shan."

Shamus Connelly and Chang Lo both knew all three stories of Ehrendhaus had been raided long ago by yobs from town and other parts and . . . others. There'd been tunnels dug into the foundation in a number of spots where they could see into the half-standing subcellars.

They saw signs posted at the edges of the fields; signs that simply said, in black letters on red, "This Area Is Patrolled." But they never saw anyone out there. The fallow fields seemed deserted, even up to the barbed wire at the edges of the noisome, desolate cornfield that no one appeared to have done anything with for about a century.

The mucky cornfield was the only way to reach the huge, remote shell of Ehrendhaus, that filthy tomb covered with nothing but mud and crumbled stone in all of what Lo called the Prime Directions. Last, he said, was nowhere, "The direction you go when you die. That's where Ehrendhaus is. On the way into the Dream."

"Would you shut it with the bloody Fu Manchu bullshit. You're giving me the creepin' willies . . . ow. Wait. Oi, lookit—"

Every now and then, they heard wild dog packs out on the promontory, as close as they ever got in their initial explorations, but the noises just cycled up and then went . . .

Nowhere. Nowhere like the holes in the ground on the edges of the woods. Holes that looked like mine vents that just went down and down and down.

Under the water was bad to look at too, even at the bare edges of the swamp where they could just make out details. Lo told him that Rock Springs, the old part of town they flooded to make Seven-Mile Lake, was still under that water, full of blue flashing lights in both cemeteries down there like the late-night musket shots of a bygone time in town.

"The bloody fuck kind of hop are you smoking, and what sort of—"

Along the eastern side of the promontory, the woods continued, stripping themselves down further and further into trash and scrub until they became Sticktown again, a village once an old logging camp built on the ragged tentacles of three older ones.

"You swear too much. Look, there's a way down and around—"

This was their trip to Ehrendhaus, begun with the smell of lilies from the half-healed scab of a front window and the pounding in the walls that began when he and Lo breached the front door, which slammed shut behind them. The trip did not end.

They remembered. Going in. The stench, weeping the juices of decomposition down the sides of every wall. Shapes like bodies lying flat on parts of the ceiling. Shapes that leaked and dripped through the floor. The way the scratching kept up and the noises came from behind every door.

Every door. So many doors. So many. Scratch. Scratch. Doors.

Doors. All the stairways that went nowhere, awful sounds coming from rooms that weren't there.

Rooms. That weren't there. But still the scratching. Scratching. Like the back bedroom on the second floor, the tiny little closed-off room with the very door painted shut, the windows boarded and sided.

The blood coating the walls from floor to ceiling up there where the stairs didn't quite reach. To Shamus, the house felt older than Pap-Pap's, which was the oldest house he knew and only built fifty years ago, before he could conceive of anyone being alive.

Shamus Connelly's brain went somewhere else. Like it did when there was trouble. He just kept remembering. And looking. He didn't flinch. He didn't cry. He didn't run. By God, they were detectives.

The memory took him, right where he stood. He remained where he was and let it. It was a grand one, at that . . .

Back when Grandma Dot was still up and about, before her circulation kept her in the rocking chair most of the time, wide-eyed against the little slices of sleep . . .

Her wide blue eyes, Dorothy Connelly's *née* Cohen's eyes that looked straight into the black, gaping, cyclopean maw of death one night when Shamus couldn't sleep.

He was staying over at Pap-Pap and Grandma Dot's big old house. That week there was two of the uncles in and out, crashing there for the night on construction gigs, and his da' so far out on the piss that his ma' was sleeping on a cot in the parlor below Shamus.

The boy was up for too long that night, ruminating about his shiner and everything he'd done that was his fault to cause, everything he should confess to

Father Skorupan about at school when he heard Confessions each Friday. From these humble ruminations, the longer he stayed awake, the more he understood the transitory, finite nature of human life.

For the first time, Shamus realized that he was going to *be* in a hole in the ground, somewhere, no matter what he did or thought or said. No matter what.

He'd cracked a rock layer of supposition while thinking about something entirely unrelated. The thought scared him half out of his wits, so very badly that he lay and twisted and sweated through nightmares until . . .

Until he padded down the upstairs hall at Ehrendhaus behind Lo, the wallpaper glittering around him in the moonlight. Far away across the street in another world, Dom McGreen's radio was still on. He knew the song. It was Duke Ellington and His Orchestra's, "Don't Get Around Much Anymore," the one without the words and . . .

And and and he crawled into bed with Grandma Dot and poured out his heart to her in tears.

She sat up in the white cotton nightshirt she always wore, looking just like she did any other time of the day, only sleepier, and she said in her gloriously inflected voice, "Pray on it, Shamus, my dear one. Pray to the Lord, for the Lord will show you the way 'round that black gapin' pit that yeh *niver* stumble into yerself, no matter if yeh dug it or not, when yeh let the Father Almighty turn on the lights and teach youse a little *humility* before it. Bow before it, and Him, and you'll live."

So saying, she curled him in her arms, stroking his hair and taking both his small, poor hands in her one big, callused, warm one, the way she did since he was a baby. "Think how many stars there are in the sky, my dear one. Each one of those is a whole world, just like unto this one, and on each one, God the Father has some sort of doin'. Now imagine how many of those He's got t'keep track of. Now how big are you, Shamus Connelly? Eh, love? How big?"

How big. How big. Big enough to not even pray, not even think, when the floor of Ehrendhaus began to shake and the horrible thing began making itself known. When crockery rattled somewhere in some cupboard and a very tall, oddly shaped man with no face—

But he had a face. But it was just . . . Shamus couldn't see a face in all that awful. He . . . it . . . the thing . . . dear God . . .

"How big are you, Shamus?"

Big enough to lock up Lo's arm like a bouncer giving a drunk the bum's rush. Big enough to crash them through an upstairs window and break his own collarbone when they hit.

"How big?"

Big enough to bark them both into a run. All the way home. Neither boy was even grounded. But it was years before they could speak of it.

THE WHITE LOTUS UNION

Father Ronson stood before the blackboard, picking up the chalk and beginning to write as he spoke.

"You will recall from Friday that Rock Springs Village was a key shipping point for the Transcontinental Railroad. In fact, it was the *nexus* of the railroad for some time, particularly during the Civil War."

Someone in the second row farted loudly. The priest's face didn't even twitch. "The PRR provided a fairly safe means of transportation over the Allegheny Ridge. After Locke Curve was built, the Allegheny Portage Railroad was no longer necessary. For quite some time, folks, this area was the proverbial electrician's J-box between industrial interests on our own coast and the more agrarian economies blooming in the West."

His words flowed into a yellow outline on the board with the speed of a stenographer or a mathematician. "'Nother little-known fact . . . people in this area had been talking union since about 1848. How many of you know when the first unions began to take hold elsewhere in America?"

The chalk froze. Shamus Connelly looked up. "1890s. United Mine Workers of America, down there . . . where all the coal mines are. Cambria County. I always forget and say the Irish word."

Father grinned warmly. "Excellent. Yes. Cambria. Welsh for *coal*, by the way. I understand your own father and grandfather were quite pivotal in the mines. My brother too. He was a shop-steward and a check-weighman. Good men." He looked at the floor. "This area was somewhat of a . . . well, I wouldn't call it a hotbed, but . . . times were hard here. Still are. People talked a lot. Not like now."

He turned back around. "How many of your fathers get silicosis pensions? Black lung, that is?" A few hands went up.

"The mines around here were booming during the States' War. Booming. There was no shortage of people eager to subject themselves to the vilest abuse. If you got black lung, you were laid off without pay. Going on 'Relief,' or mine unemployment, took several months to file for."

Outside the window, the graveyard was a crenellated maze of cedar trees whose slope fell nearly straight down in a perfect angle. Father forced himself to look away from the sun hanging high in the sky.

"Takes weeks now," young Sascha Turman lisped hesitantly from the back row. "That's what my papa said. It was five weeks before those b—" His face reddened. "He said it was five weeks before they came to call."

"Indeed," Father's face grew more severe. "And the Lord forgives you the pithy word you were going to use. " (Sascha smiled and relaxed.) "You worked from dawn to dusk in those mines, and if you complained about anything back then, there was no grievance process. You just got sent on down the road."

Father looked wistful. "Freethinker spirit at the local level seems long extinct. Here . . ." He flapped one hand. He'd lost them.

The picture displayed behind him on the blackboard was a big old daguerreotype, probably done with one of those big cameras up on poles like Jimmy Hennessy's dad had in the back of his pawnshop in Germantown. It showed a long factory building on familiar soil. The stone eyes of union workmen glared out from the foreground.

The folded-armed proletariat wore greasy long johns and coveralls. The men had on galluses and tool belts. Many of their legs were game, twisted or missing, wearing the blue woolen trousers of former Federal infantry.

The workmen wore their hair long, sideburns and garrison caps and ponytails, beards past their chins shot with gray and blasted with scars. Many of the front line looked like they were under eighteen. In the back, off to the side, was a haughty-looking Chinese woman dressed like a Union soldier, brandishing a sawed-off shotgun that looked as big as a locomotive axle.

"Rock Springs," Shamus muttered. "The Foundry Strike. The one my father called"—he snapped his fingers—"Little Haymarket. That woman in the front there, they called her Shotgun Annie. Annie Chang . . ."

"Shamus," the good father asked hesitantly, "could you repeat all that for the rest of the class?"

They were still talking when the bell rang.

THE BAREFOOT-DOCTOR

Shamus met his greatest teacher on a muggy summer day with the river up and sluggish and the bugs out in droves. He saw freshwater squid in some of the gutters that were overflowing on a block here and a block there on the way down to Chang's Drugstore with the saloon out back.

Most of the squid were dead, but one wasn't. That one was gone quick, down a storm drain before he had time to even make a noise.

That was the summer Shamus first learned to appreciate walking everywhere for the sheer joy of walking on a good day, meeting Lo halfway to play dice or cards or smoke sloppily rolled cigarettes on long hikes while they argued the merits of older cars that were easier to work on.

"But Model T's can so run on alky-hol. My da' ran that flivver he kept on the dregs from his still . . ."

The Monongahela ruins were on the other side of Potter's Ridge from Demarest Hospital. Lo swore they were Manchurian, or at least, some of the characters in the stones were the same. "See," he pointed at the trilithon he was leaning against just then. "And . . . but why is the cloth radical *there*. It wouldn't—"

"But it's my folk fit the stones together to make walls like this," Shamus interrupted, standing over him and looking at a different edge of the arch.

"My people make walls too," Lo said, trying not to smile. "There's this great big one I read about once, and . . ."

Shamus punched him on the arm with the flat, rubber part of one glove. "Listen, smartass. I bet this is a Dream-place. You feel it? Shut up once. You will."

Lo did, closed his eyes, and linked his fingers with the indexes pointed out and up. He seemed to be breathing more slowly, and the color in his face improved. A small, ironic smile etched its way across his cheeks not more than a minute later. He mumbled something in Mandarin and opened his eyes.

"We're not supposed to be here." The smile never left his face. "This is a killing ground." He pantomimed choking. "From the inside out. You—"

Shamus wasn't buying it. "Wanna go climb the bony-pile?"

Lo looked like he was shaking something off. "Race you . . ."

Shamus almost beat him. They climbed the bony pile almost the whole way to the top and took the spiral road the miners had left the rest of the way up to the nervous knot of weeds that always looked like it was screaming and the stone in hard mud that Lo said could never be a human skull, at least not a *Homo sapiens* . . .

"You're the homo, yeh know-it-all. It's some kind of skull though. Maybe a possum or a coon . . ."

Now Lo punched *him* in the arm. "Sister says we're not supposed to say *coon* in public. It's the same thing as—"

"Shut it! Want to go see if Ma's made lunch?"

Lo shook his angular head. "Ever had fried crayfish?" he asked inscrutably. "We've leftovers in the icebox. Hundreds. They heat up nice on the stove. It . . ."

Shamus frowned, following him back to the road and the place where the sidewalk began again at the edge of the rock dump at the bottom terminus of North End Avenue.

"Aren't they *bugs*?" he chided, looking very small and pale in his wide-brimmed hat. "But I wanna meet your grandad. Didn't you say he was a sawbones?"

"Not exactly." Lo slowed down to walk beside him, his black Converse sneakers smoothly keeping pace with Shamus's own severe wingtips. "He is a wandering lama of the barefoot-doctors, who are magicians to a man. Or woman."

"Isn't that a line from *Captain Trouble*?" Shamus guessed. "I think I have that one, sure, it—"

Lo snickered. "It's true. Just wait."

Lo's grandfather lived in the back of the endlessly fascinating Wei Building, a rooming house over a seedy old tavern full of mirrors and braincases anaesthetizing themselves at the short bar where a long water spittoon in the tile flowed twinklingly on like all the years.

Shamus and Lo chased each other up four flights of winding inner-atrium hotel stairs, up through successive lines of wash from longtime residents—Mrs.

Kwan's drawers were so big that Shamus stopped dead in his tracks twice and gawked until Lo dragged him back up—to emerge at the southeast corner of the walkup out of breath, chortling like buffalo.

"Get bright," Lo told him, "or Zufu will . . . how do your people say it . . . take the piss out of you."

Shamus looked surprised. "Yer pickin' up a disturbing amount of our lingo. Planning on converting? Hell, you catch on so quick you could probably interpret for *me*."

"Are you still on about that from class?" Lo asked. "It's a bad time over there right now. Doesn't your family take the paper? They got uprisings in Ireland, and . . . we're here."

He removed his shoes, motioning that Shamus should do the same. Shamus frowned, sighed, bent, and turned his wretched hands to his shoelaces, second-least favorite task of personal hygiene with the first better imagined than described.

At length, he rose in his socks, still wearing his hat, and padded into the vast, bright apartment behind Chang Lo, shielding his eyes against the glare.

A slender, perfectly still man who looked like an incredibly ornate waxwork sat in a canvas sling chair at the far corner of the room. The whole west wall was made of windows, hung with white paper mats backed in tinfoil that diffused and reflected the glare from the whitewashed walls and roof outside.

It was economical. It was Chinese in a kind of way Shamus couldn't even explain, let alone understand. Though furnished in only the bare essentials, the vast, breezy apartment managed to convey a cozy, mellow sense of peace that he'd never experienced indoors anywhere in his life, let alone with a windchime hanging from the ceiling of the parlor.

The little Westinghouse console radio was tuned to WKLA, which was playing, for a wonder, "Exactly Like You" by the Ink Spots. In the middle of the room, perpendicular to the radio, a long, low black coffee table stretched to groaning with issues of *Life* and *Look* and *Collier's Weekly*.

The old bald barefoot-doctor sat in his chair in the middle of the room, literally barefoot, cross-legged, skinning what looked like a maple leaf just . . . so . . .

Shamus's eyes, behind the blackish lenses, zeroed in on this wonderment as the spindly fingers spun the leaf into an archer's bow in miniature, with a slender arrow nocked.

"Lai wan-le," he rasped half-jokingly at his grandson. They were speaking Mandarin, rich in various compliments unnecessary to report.

Lo took it way too seriously, rapping back, "Mei gwan'xi, zufu! Wo fei shile!" Tien flapped his free hand, shaking his head.

"Hello, Shamus," the old dragon rasped. "I'm Doc Chang, Lo's pappy." He got to his feet with a weird, fluid motion that seemed to involve his arms in no way at all. His head didn't even bob. He had a light step for a man of his apparent age.

He was an elderly gentleman dressed in a long black silk coat with purple trousers neatly tied at the ankles over his lack of socks. He wore a cap after the Mandarin fashion. There was something merry and undignified and bright about his eyes and the corners of his guileless smile that always wanted to leap out, a smile carved from old ivory.

Shamus gaped. The doc cocked his head at him, hands linked now behind his back. "Son, welcome to my home. So glad you finally came to call."

"Will you teach me Kung-fu?" he blurted. Tien looked at his grandson like he was about to make some blistering wisecrack but thought better of it. He looked at his feet.

"That would be highly unorthodox," he sighed. "Love the orthodox, or hate it, it is the traditions and the old ways of what we do that keep us honest and regular and sane." He saw he was losing the boy, made himself think differently, and then spoke again.

"I was never a monk. But I have healed many monks in my day. The Shaolin like to trade. To teach a little." He looked at the floor. "I know some Kung-fu, a little kara-te. But it's . . . not done, not this way, it . . ."

Lo cleared his throat from the couch. "He means no gwai-los can play."

Shamus's heart twisted in half like a beer can and died. The doc looked sad. "No, no, no, just . . . they haven't before." He was thinking very quickly. "I have many things to give you. Let's start with the basics," he snickered at Lo again, like the boy had narrowly avoided a long lecture. "Kung-fu is lovely. And beautiful. And fun," His eyes grew hard. Proud. "But if you want to be calm and happy, we have to start from the ground."

Shamus was still lost but in a more positive sense. "Fair enough. Ma' says I put the cart before the horse."

Doc Chang nodded, looking more closely at Shamus's face, like he'd missed something. "Oh, yes . . . the library." His eyes grew misty. "She knows Han Shan.

And Li Po. Not in the original, of course. But . . . yes, Anna understands about poetry. Now I see why. May I . . . may I have a look at those hands of yours, please? Forgive an old busybody. I'll give you a whole silver dollar if you let me make some sketches of them, take a few notes. With your full permission, of course. I don't need to do anything but look and draw. I'll only examine them if you allow it."

Shamus thought about that. "What is it yeh want to know about 'em? Had 'em all my life," he couldn't hide the grin, "Don't know no different, but I'd imagine if you just started out now wi'em' it'd be a terrible pain in the arse."

Doc Chang roared with laughter, smacking his hands together (the way, Shamus thought, Pap-Pap would demonstrate a "knee-slapper"). "You have a fine mind. Welcome to our home. Lo was just going to insist you stay for dinner."

Shamus goggled helplessly. Doc Chang didn't.

"Shamus, I can help you manage your pain. I can't make it go away, but I can teach you how to turn it into . . ."

He was holding Shamus's hands up, palpating the inner and outer spirals of knuckles. Shamus didn't protest. Doc Chang's hands felt no different than Dr. Drebel's own cool, dry, impersonal ones.

"Well, I don't know exactly," he admitted, "I'm surprised you can get anywhere near a light bulb or"—he sighed—"have you ever read of Nikola Tesla?"

"Pap-Pap thinks he's the bee's knees," Shamus shook his head. "I dunno, he . . ."

"There's a few books I want to let you read," Tien mused. "I . . . I'm what you call a, well, like a like a country doctor. I work with the Cantonese and Manchu around here who road-gang on the PRR. Please close your eyes."

Shamus did and gasped. The old man was doing something to his hands.

His own dry, careful hands didn't touch the skin, but the pain went up and out and out again and . . . Doc Chang was making noises like a strong man lifting a big block of stone.

It sounded like the block kept getting bigger and bigger, but . . . like he *liked* to lift it in a way. Like lifting it was helping *him*.

Then he just *stopped* and made strange gestures at the windows with his hands. The silence thickened around the house as he spoke. His rich voice gained a dreamy, childlike clarity.

"Chi-kung," he explained, bowing mysteriously at the window. "Fear is but wisdom in its germinal cause, Shamus. It is all right to be afraid. I can *move* fear and pain. We all can, not just us old guys. Hell, the kung-fu masters back home have been doing it for thousands of years."

Shamus looked up as the sunlight caught the razor steel between the slats of the two bright silk fans on the wall. He wondered what he was walking into and decided it was better than anything on *The Shadow* ever was, and that was his favorite program, so this was the best.

"Can you teach me how to cloud men's minds?" he asked, trying to look serious. Doc Chang processed the question for a moment, made a rude noise, and gave him the finger.

"Sure, just stand them a round of Irish whiskey," he scoffed. "But I *can* teach you how to use your own mind to the fullest. How to wake up in your dreams and heal your spirit . . . and make a bully kick his own ass."

After a moment, Shamus remembered to shut his mouth. "My ancestors really were magicians, not just humble pestle pounders such as me." Doc Chang smiled expansively. "They lived out in the Gobi Desert for years at a time and traveled as nomads. They called themselves the People of the Dark and sought to hone the edge of abilities that all people had in the earlier ages of the world, those abilities lost due to science. Being able to read the color of a man's soul, Shamus, and tell him how to get well. Being able to balance a spirit . . . or stop a heart . . . with your hands."

Shamus was looking at a weird heathen idol by the window, pale blue as a thunderhead. It looked like a man with a halo, rather like Our Lord Jesus, seated cross-legged and rising from his chair. Doc Chang noted the distraction, which was truly no distraction at all.

"Mi-leh-fu will come again, the Rigden Djappo of the mountain sages on the Plains of Leng. The new Prince of Peace, the Maitreya. The Lord of Light for whom Past and Future are but different towns, side by side in the same direction . . ."

Chang answered Shamus's snaggle-toothed gape with a smile and an upraised forefinger. "Ah?"

For that, Shamus had no ready answer.

. . . AND ALL WAS LIGHT

Dusk in a northern town with fried chicken smelling delicious three blocks away, competing awfully with the paper mill and burning leaves and the whippoorwill whistle of the wind out where he was. Out where he might not ought to have been with that purpose. But.

But. Shamus knew that he was getting stirred up needlessly. His hands were hurting the wrong way. He wanted to turn and run, but something rooted him to the spot and made his head hurt.

He twisted around, twisted through the bolt of pain in his head and pulled something up and out—the way he felt Tien pull his pain up and out before—and the wave swept along the floor, up and out, and the power came back on up and out.

And out again. Out of the rotting sea of Crestview rooftops and back alleys, out in the yard, the soft storm wind sprang up, tickling him behind his big ears, making him pay attention. Making him . . .

Shamus shifted uncomfortably, letting his rock-hard member lay along his belly. *Aw brilliant,* he thought disparagingly. *Just like last time. It'll be two hours and more before you can piss again, and . . .*

But even his annoying boner was far away. Inside, he felt that cold nothing as the shadows grew around him and a few birds up in the maples made confused sounds out of the deep silence. The clouds were boiling. The ground knew something he didn't: the lines of force, the sacred magnetism, the field of the planetary dynamo. In this antique light, there were no creatures arguing. Shamus closed his eyes, knelt, and began to breathe.

"TO ME!!!" he screamed, forgetting everything.

But slowly, gathering from the feet up and down, the clouds answered, *Yes.* The snap stomped the yard flat and smacked the ground solid. He was deaf. He would be deaf. Damn it. *Oww.* It felt like a baby had its foot in either ear.

The boom rolled off the hills and houses and his smoking palms, full of sound and fury and signifying all the head-down baffled rage that cooped him in that neighborhood, that room, that storm, that migraine, that gathering . . .

Shamus Connelly was on his knees. His hands were smoking and black. And the smile reached either jug ear. "Thanks be to God," was Shamus's only comment on the matter.

He was back at Chang's that night, feeling as full as a paintbrush, a pen, the calligraphy sables of the doc's Chinese poets he had no heart to read until then, there on the wild Hou Shan, the mountainous Feng-ti-Yu, Valley of Hell . . .

The doc was a barrel of fun to be around, and after the first year of getting his hands worked on, Shamus wanted to wring his neck. But he learned to listen, to reflect. He learned the Buddhist tenet that all release comes at the moment of exhale, or as Doc Tien admonished, "Hold your breath and squeeze."

Then he'd make him dip his hand in a glass of water with a needle mounted on the outside and watch his watch. Shamus wondered mildly what kind of research paper all this would produce but left it alone.

He was just there for the pao-tzu tarts. Manifestly, there was famine but rarely in the house of Chang Tien. After a while, when they started in with what the doc knew of the fighting arts, the old man moved the few items of furniture to the back room. Soon enough, Shamus began to learn how to make an attacker lose . . .

BEGINNING OF THE END

(Undated Entry —CB)

I don't know why writing all this stuff down does so much good. But Doc Tien knows what he's doing.

The Doc says I'm a healer or will be. I'd settle for just being able to own a pair of shoes with laces that I could tie instead of those ghastly buckles that always pinch the balls of my second thumbs.

Every night, I dream I'm being hauled off to jail like in that hillbilly song by Jimmie Rodgers. Every morning, it doesn't happen. I can only assume that God hasn't gotten me this far just to drop me on my poor head again.

But if only anyone knew. The further back I look in my journals—I've been keeping since I was five . . . heavens. What am I? What have I been allowed to be, and what, pray tell, is to come?

I'm not a monster. I know what the tests said. I know what a genius really is . . . and what it really isn't. I'm smart enough to not go off half-cocked about it, but they still didn't tell me.

I had to swipe the envelope out of Ma's bureau drawer and see for myself that I was never retarded or feeble at all. Only deformed. Differently enabled, if you like. Differently human.

The family knows all of what I am. They know all of what I can do. They just don't want to believe anything that's right in front of them. If they did, they might remember that there's a whole other language they've never learned to read, one of personal revelation instead of blind slavery, an alphabet . . .

An alphabet of lightning. I dream about a *true* monster—not a thing like me at all, a true boggart. The Man with No Face. Lord of the Dead, Lord of Pleasure Island, who comes for me, yanking me around town in my sleep, telling me all the filth that men do.

I don't have to participate or even watch. Just listen and turn my head when . . .

But the Man with No Face says these are shades of things that had been and have no consciousness of us any way round. He knows his Dickens, the old monstrosity. I wonder what he looked like when he was a person.

The Man with No Face is kind of yellow-green. He wears a top hat and an emerald ring. He seems to fade in and out like a funhouse mirror when you look at him: now an earnest young man with spiky red hair much like mine, now a sick old thing, bescaled, *aware*.

Those dreams aren't all that nice. But they seem to toughen me if only because getting out of bed and firing up the percolator becomes an act of the purest and most delicious freedom imaginable when I am loosed from the iron grip of that saprophytic vine.

Live or die by the boogeyman's slow hand, at least I got to play Mr. Electrico at the school Science Fair last year. Lo and I worked up to that for a bit.

I *had* the room then. No matter how I had to do it, I *had* them. For the first time, girls were looking at me like something besides a sideshow act. I danced the big ball of what Mr. Tesla calls tele-force through my fingers, the big lightning-critter whirligig twisting, twirling, wanting to fly, wanting to pop.

Keeping the serpent of fire down near my spine, I spun it into a bow and skipped rope with a twenty-thousand-volt arc . . . then began to do the double Dutch with Lo. (He kept his game face on and slick. We'd rehearsed several times, though he insisted on wearing the thickest-soled pair of gym shoes he could scrape together the couch change from the doc's to go and buy.)

Woomph. I took off Pap-Pap's hat and took a bow. The hat was smoking. I was smoking. I wasn't allowed to smoke on school property. I wondered madly if Headmaster Neugebauer would say anything.

"There you have it," Lo said quietly from the tiny podium in front of me. "Potential uses of the electron, brought to you by Mr. Electrico himself. Thanks for watching."

"I have no idea what applications this would have," Brother Bernard, the Franciscan monk who taught our Applied Science course that year, stammered into the applause, "but how'd you kids do it? Anodized discs or . . ."

"Ancient Chinese secret!" Lo wisecracked. "I'll show you the blueprints, Brother. All . . . uhh, perfectly harmless."

The monk looked slightly mollified. "Fair enough, lads. That was"—he scratched his chin—"that was divinely inspired madness. Have either of you ever thought about applying for the Governor's Honors in Sciences Program? New program they instituted out of Harrisburg . . ." Some things, for good or ill, were invariably lost in the shuffle.

Mum always tells me we have the gift of the Fey in such a way that I take it to be a good thing. She swears upon her own sainted mum's bones— Godrestersoulfathersonholyghost amen—that I told her where to find the old photo album up in the back attic, the one we didn't use for much but stuff Mum and Papa had when they first came over from the old sod.

Mum swears I found it for her when I was two and hadn't ever been up there. To me, everyone in this family just has this freakish memory that's too much for their own damn good if you ask me, which few ever do.

But I always associated Mum's talk of the Fey with my flip-books I made in school, which became stories and not just stories but then tales, the kind where the words reach up from the page and grip you hard enough to quiver.

I associated the Fey with the flickery yellow light in the cellar Pap-Pap and his brothers built, on the steep wooden stairs, descending to the dirt floor fragrant with Cutty Pipe tobacco, that tiny labyrinth in stone and mortar that I could walk blindfolded, that warm catacomb of broken foundations hauled over from the yoke of moving to and fro at the mercy of the colliery bond in northern England.

The coalfields. The big smoke. The fires that burned men from their homes and mums and babbies . . .

Pap-Pap's house has roots much further than most would suppose. There are three different sections of cellar, clearly delineated from oldest to newest by the construction of the stone walls. Back and to the right, up under the stairs, is the oldest. The mortar holding the fitted stones of that section of wall together is easily 1900 at the earliest, little more than an oatmeal of native ingenuity.

As a child's index finger traces outward from the center of the cellar, running along the chinks in those stones, the mortar solidifies, coheres, becoming smoother and stronger. The stones' rough edges mill themselves a bit.

Closer to the area of the workbench and the porte cochere, the cinderblocks in the side wall speak of steady, constant construction and clarification, making ready for a family, a new block of neighbors, to breathe life into those stones: love and laugh, sweat and bleed there, work and play and pray and read and weep.

I feel it all just going down those stairs, down into the roots of 1137 Grant

Street, the Tree of the World, dug into the hillside not to mine out but only expose a rich and golden vein that the dead sticks of words can barely get all the way round.

You go up one landing and down one to get to the coal bin that provides the heat for that big old house during the brutally cold Callaight County winters, wherein we stuff every hole in every wall with a rag and drip wax on it just to keep it neat and then park a bookshelf in front of it and burn another old article of clothing rather than a book.

We never go hungry, but certain facts cross all boards. Tucked away in the first nook behind the first set of stairs is Mum's big silver bowl for making bread in the woodstove in the kitchen. Pap-Pap taught me to bank and tend the bread-fire when I got a little bigger.

Time was, I always kept the kindling box full on the back porch to bring in for Grandma Dot, so she could fire up the stove. There's a separate woodpile in the front of the coal room, down into that damp earthen smell with all the coffee cans in all the nooks and crannies like some kind of industrial catacomb. I still do that, but the routines are all long changed.

No part of the machine is ever wasted here. The stove smells best, the wood as fresh as bread, the bread the breath of God. It's worth getting your hands dirty, every last time.

I know they're getting on in years, but I hope to God we have them around for a while. They let me write here all I want. They let me *be*.

(later entry)

On the other side of Spruce Street from Our Lady is the Grant Street graveyard, genesis of so many daydreams for me, staring out the window in class far away down in the bowl of the valley. That was before the view got built over, and there was nothing to draw the eye away from that impossible perspective of century oaks and mausoleums.

In all those daydreams, the necropolis of town added up to something more. All them stone tally marks finally meant something. All those lives ended up having been given not in vain but for some distant other purpose, chasing itself away over the hills, falling toward town from the stars.

I wanted so badly to touch what I saw in those daydreams, to turn it over in my hands . . .

And found myself left only with me own self, standing in freezing winds at the edge of a black wrought-iron fence, looking over that snow-filled cradle where I hatched.

I could write for days about this, on or off the medicine in the arm or the wee little codeine syrup bottle. All the life that most folks think there is to lead is only mimicry of the fossil footsteps in the rocks beneath them roads here. They toss their bodies onto the bonfire whose ashes generated this land, piling the ruins higher still.

I scare that sort all half to death, to the last man jack among them. They see me seeing right through them to all that poison inside like railroad slop hidden in the sewers, waiting to bubble up and flood the streets.

I only see such colors as those ordinarily here in town every Fourth of July, in fact. Every memory of fireworks, as Chang Lo clutches his sack of bottle rockets and gushes in Cantonese, and I crack up laughing and roll around on the grass.

How proud I am to be an American, celebrating independence with mock artillery stolen from the Chinese, celebrating wars and jails. The smell has gotten into my clothes. Gunpowder sparks flash through my name with a sparkler, Tom Sawyer-style on the street.

When I was about five, me and Ma' went to the top of the Grant Street graveyard to watch the fireworks. Same place we used to go to watch the Perseids when we couldn't get up to St. Basil's, that wonderful foggy bit of street corner I always end up sleepwalking to—or used to.

She told me I cried at the end, "It's over . . . it's over." With the benefit of long hindsight, I realized that I was talking about America.

Fireworks blare through the sky in my head, in cobwebs of smoke that somehow remain where they are, breaking my train of thought. There are always broken bottles in the graveyard and songs of unjust death down at the bar.

Bury the whole damned rotten carnival of town at their feet, and if *(here a name is crossed out—CB)* the liar politician should wake and find his slaves in his tomb, he will eat them alive and do us all a favor.

From the tip-top of the cemetery hill, one funny hollow child looks out at town, ruling all he surveys. A hard, ancient light flares in his eyes, the place where combustion begins.

Remember when the roofline was something to be contemplated for hours while you swam in the lawn? Remember the simple days when you didn't have to hurtle pell-mell, didn't have to be nowhere for nothing?

Ma' taught me to love and honor the times when the mind is free to play. Ma' took me to the college for my very first time when I was thirteen. She was still finishing her coursework in secondary education on the parish's dime, and good for her.

Ma' took me up there on the wheezing, old-school shuttle trolley, the one that smelled like a library. We brought a picnic hamper with Moxies and ham sandwiches and big, thick cookies, and we sat out behind the English Department on the old ballfield in them rickety bleachers and watched the Perseid meteors cycle into life that night in the star field overhead.

All of them fell faster and faster, far from the madding lights of town, making me ache through and through with the suffocating consciousness of their journey.

Ma' taught me everything, then and now. How to make terribly clever monkey faces at breakfast with an orange slice in your mouth, when oranges could be had. How to read when I was four. Ma' was an angel . . .

There were no words except in his head, the doc talking him through one form or the other in the tai chi chuan. Words out of time itself, into space, echoing around the rasp of a big manila envelope being opened by a horny, vestigial nail on a finger that has no name.

"Ma', I . . . got accepted at St. Basil's for criminal justice. I can be a . . . detective, like you always said I might do."

He was nearly hopping up and down like a little kid about to wee in his pants. "Pinkerton takes work-study students all the time from that major, the friar said, and . . . and—"

"My boy," Anna beamed softly, crossing the room to take his hands in hers and waltz him around until they were both roaring with laughter . . .

As well, Shamus remembered all the things he couldn't remember in the long months of preparing for school. He didn't leave his room at all for a day or two after he arrived.

Shamus wrote a lot and left most of his meals outside his room, uneaten, much as he would when school finally started and the campus of St. Basil's began to shun him or adopt him, fifty-fifty by clique and individual.

He went through a string of roommates, most of them blind or in wheelchairs and between off-campus apartments somewhere else. He didn't mind. His room was on the ground floor of Wallace Hall, and he had a fine view of the woods. With so much time to himself, he barely knew the half of what to do with it.

Shamus didn't know how he felt any more about much of anything, and that was the most hellish part. Someone would tell him how he was supposed to feel at some point. At the moment, this was about the best he could do.

Those first few weeks at St. Basil's were the most Beat weeks of his life, spent half-awake in low, droning underground classrooms full of asbestos checkerboard tile and weird smells, taking notes on procedure and discretion and a hundred other different kinds of words he never wanted to hear again.

Shamus wanted to be on the street. He wanted to be a sleuth. This criminal justice stuff was for punks. The Dream showed him who he really was, who was really inside him, so much bigger than this world where he was a grown man stuck at a desk and reciting by rote.

He was a soldier in his dreams, a peacemaker, a tactician and technician who plumbed the depths of the human soul . . . but his day job was at least of some interest.

Being a Pinkerton security guard at Powersburg First National Bank gave Shamus at least a chance to study people, more than any stale, boring class full of legal jargon and old-fogy logic ever could. He made them laugh. He asked after their mothers. He cared about what they said.

Shamus taught them how a polydactyl person flipped the bird, where the best places were in town to eat . . . and what to do with someone having a heart attack or choking on something or any other weird thing he'd read about at the doc's. He gave them a smile they might not have known they could make, any one of them or two who passed through those doors, even when nothing happened, which was most of the time.

He gave them something else to look at. He took the piss out of them. He gave them lightning.

HIGHER GROUND

It was nearly the close of business on Christmas Eve, 1948, a mad boom time that only touched Callaight County a little. Everyone in Powersburg was hurrying home.

Little kids hauled each other on new Sears sleds down the street, metal runners hissing in the snow. Even the traffic cop Burke McTarnahan's eyes surreptitiously twinkled as he caught a snowflake on his tongue here and there when he thought no one was looking.

The wind kicked up. At the corner, below the big wreath on the streetlight, the decorative plastic Santa, cracking the whip over Rudolph and the whole nine, busted its bolt and sailed off a ways down the telephone-wire as though the runner of Santa's sleigh were a real sleigh-runner, for almost a full minute, before it fell to earth. (Burke howled with laughter and wrote it up.)

"Ding Dong Merrily on High" ding-donged merrily with the volume on high from every brand-new Philco radio behind the plate glass of Wyler's Home Furnishings Emporium in the old white-brick firehouse at Main Street and Asylum Avenue, next door to the bank.

No one in town was buying new radios much, so all the radios had to stay there in the orphanage for Christmas, sounding the clangor and the screaming of the bells out into the burning copper sky. Gigantic snowflakes spun and tumbled, dumping down in sheets. It was four in the afternoon and already dark. The bank was open for one more hour.

Sgt. Jack Yoder, US Army-Ret., wasn't going there to take out a loan to buy a radio though. He wasn't even interested in the free toaster. After Korea, after the front and the whole shitshow after that, his mind was full of only snow.

Much of his life got chewed out of him in a thousand sunsets at absolute zero in snow much like this, on the rim of the world twenty klicks from anywhere and a thousand light years past the sun, where they burned shit to stay warm and ate barbecued greyhound and rotten cabbage, where all the locals ever called him was GI when they weren't telling stories about storm-dragons coming down from the skies to repel invaders from all directions

Now he was on patrol—just on patrol all the time now, crossing Main and Canal, noting the edge of the curb that was already buried. Now he was wearing four sweaters and three pairs of fatigue pants, all layered together like flak gear, a flannel hat with earflaps, and a clear plastic false face across the front. The party mask came from HL Green's, mere blocks away, and really didn't look a thing like Errol Flynn. More like a mustachioed Georgie Jessel.

Condensation was building up inside the mask. He didn't care. He was on patrol. Jack was on patrol and ding-donging along in his head, ding-dong, to the dinging and the ringing of the dong, merrily on high, and there were lights and tinsel and motorized angels dancing in the window of the furniture store just presently. Outside Green's, a skinny junkie in a Santa suit coughed and spat and rang his bell. Jack nearly stumbled over him.

"Hey, Merry Christmas. Fight tuberculosis, folks—" the junky said, looking at his bucket.

"Get stuffed," Jack snarled back, shoving him out of the way. In his pocket, he fingered the Purple Heart.

In his wallet, he knew, the eviction notice burned and burned and him with it, and the blaze was so hot he didn't know what his left hand was doing. Powersburg First National towered over the block as artless as its sign, as stone-gray foreboding as the county jail or the old state hospital.

Jack remembered he got thrown out of there last week by Corey the morning guard for obscenity after the loan officer called him indigent and Jack called him a few things that had a few more syllables. For a moment, the line let him in and stuffed him in the back of the snaking intestine of people: the guy with the white cane, the woman with the baby wrapped in a blanket at her shoulder.

Jack looked at her sourly. The kid was probably old enough to verbally demand the tit. Someone in back of him made an Errol Flynn joke, but there wasn't really time to slap her down. The guard was a floater, a fill-in, someone he didn't know. Definitely not the young guy who never took off his gloves. Unknown quantity. In any case, it was time to make a hole. Joe shucked the shotgun as he drew it from his coat in one clean motion and blew away that fat-assed guard.

"GET ON THE GROUND, MOTHER FUCKERS!" he screamed. "THIS IS A HOLDUP!" The guard was only just in the process of landing on said ground.

The noise his body made when it did so was a noise of dead weight only, no brain behind the motion.

The three tellers shrank back when Jack drew near, panting in the mask, heart racing, nose full of the smells of burning shit and roasting dog, the smells of Korea where he left part of his right foot and most of his mind.

There was a mad dash for the exit. Jack reloaded, firing once more into the air. The diaspora out into the snow roughly paused halfway. That was bad. That meant notice.

He really wouldn't have much time now, but the tellers already had a pretty good idea what he was after. One of them he knew; her ringlets didn't have any gray. She knew his eyes, and her own teared up, but Meg kept right on stoically shoving money into anything around that looked like a bag: paper sacks from Green's, the guts of two old leather briefcases, even a black Glad trash bag to hold the lot.

The bank door hadn't closed. Jack turned his head, irritated, about to wave one of the herd up off the ground with both barrels to go and—

"PINKERTON DETECTIVE!" the newcomer, a young man with a mismatched .38 automatic in either hand, bellowed as he'd clearly been taught to bellow. There was a paycheck sticking out of his pocket, shoved there like a Kleenex in the moment. "DROP THE CANNON NOW, SARGE! YOU ARE RELIEVED OF DUTY! YOU—"

But Shamus's buddies who were "fit for service" had often told him that NCOs weren't known much for negotiating. Pap-Pap's Fedora tilted back on Shamus's head as his spiky red hair began to stand up straight as the whack whack whack, the dance of fire and return fire, shut his mouth before he stuck both size-thirteen wingtips right in.

For a reeling second, while the nightmare truth of what he was seeing flared in his brain, Shamus longed for death. Then in a frenzy of action, he was his fighting self for the first time.

"Oh, sod this," he growled in the smoke and mess as Jack looked madly around for him through people bolting for the exits. The mother with the baby in arms was most of the way to the door when Jack missed her by a good half a foot with both barrels.

Sprayed with smoking splinters, the young blonde hit the deck, clutching her son in both arms, and rolled behind the big display of potted ferns by the front window. That was all the distraction Shamus needed. This was *his* bank, his paycheck, his . . . dammit, he was . . .

"Bull of the Woods." Shamus lowered his head, raised his hands to the sky, stood still, and charged up. "I'm the Bull of the Woods around here."

Charged with the power of the shield before which even the sword trembled, as Doc Chang always said when he wanted to go run out somewhere and get his edge snapped off.

Not so now. Now the charge was stationary and refused to dissipate. His hands were screaming like scalded cats. The pistols were hot, and that two-handed hot dog shite really was for the movies and no more. Jimmy Cagney never broke his wrists in the movies either, Shamus thought dourly, or had to put up with half of this.

Both twisted hands holstered his loaner work-irons as he lowered his head. By the time Jack saw him coming, the sarge was completely unmanned, mask hanging half off his face where the elastic melted, melted, melted, and . . .

Then the Errol Flynn face, the clear gag mask of a type all the rage that year it seemed, began to shrink onto his face with the charge, charge, charge gathering around him at full speed, gathering above his head, wanting the ground . . .

The ground. The ground. The ground. The kid was taking off his gloves. The kid was looking at him. Jack knew that look from gooks hopped up on speed, charging at him over sandbags and bodies and waving Chinese rifles.

He'd seen that look on plenty of white men too, just never directed at him and certainly never from a *cripple*. That look wanted to reach down Jack's throat and pull out his guts. It was a look that forgot to be afraid to die.

Inside the bank, just before it all ended, it smelled like rain for some reason. Like rain . . . and hot plastic.

In two quick strokes, Dr. Drebel's black gloves were off, and Shamus's terrible hands encircled Jack's neck. The heart attack was over in seconds, and the Sisters of Mercy remanded the sarge to one of Chief Reed's holding cells two miles away at the Borough Building as soon as he was upright and taking nourishment.

Not one cop on the force interrogated Shamus Connelly that night. Few got near him. One of them ran him out a beer. He drank it at a draught. Another one crossed himself. All three of them spoke not a word between them. None were necessary.

WORKING-CLASS HERO

I never had to work again after the citation for bravery from the Pinkerton Agency, after Reed and the Chamber of Commerce did for me old mither in ways that she wouldn't hear of at first until she saw what the new bankbook looked like.

I invested the money. Mostly. Some of it, I just plain blew on a new black Hudson Hornet—that year's model!—a few suits of clothes, and enough beer and whiskey and tea to stand the whole town a round.

And a new hat. Not a new kind of hat. Just a new hat, just like Pap-Pap's only without the scorch marks. Mr. Helmer (with the perfect name) custom-fitted it for me at that little haberdashery of his on the town diamond, and I spent the whole day at the pizza parlor next door afterward daydreaming about Pap-Pap and Bogey flicks and the times that were and will always be.

But I was in school. I had things to do. The money would get me far for a few years if I kept the head about me I always had, all Pap-Pap's talk of *make do* and *make work*. And I thought I'd shed my kid-fears when I got to college.

But I knew all the gilded, creaking, formalin-smelling crevices and oddments of the old monastery-school better than St. Basil's own administration. I feel everything. The electricity in the wires in the walls, the way people build up a charge. Sometimes it hurts when some people so much as speak.

But I can feel their true feelings too. And their thoughts. I've been practicing. Nobody wants to play poker with me anymore or bet on so much as the weather. They get it. In Powersburg, I'm just one more freak in someone else's sideshow. So it went.

I rarely slept without a bromo or codeine. My hands ached blind fire when fall came. So did my spine.

One early morning, I was up, hunched for warmth over some excremental coffee from the common room, ignoring a suspicious piece of Danish.

When just as it began to rain cold and hard, this rocket crashed through my window, fell to my rug, smoked a bit like rotten eggs and brimstone, and fizzled right out. I waited for it to go boom, but it was clearly not a dud firework or a toy. It just kept smoking.

Nervously I poured a bit of cold coffee on it and kept on smoking, myself, clenching the sweet Herbert Tareyton in my teeth and typing with my other hand. I'd sort the mess later. I had two big papers due, and it wasn't even Wednesday. I—

Forced myself into the moment, the way Doc Chang always suggested I do when I clearly have my head up my own arse. I sensed a presence . . . nearer. Footsteps thundered up the hall.

Single set of footsteps, dead set on something. A girl. A . . . woman. All woman. Dead set on righting something. A witchy sort of girl, one you look at and just know. I was in bits. I was done. There was no one like her.

"Oh my God, I am so sor—" Cricket Bennigan began.

I held up one hand, gloveless, and she gasped.

"T'ink naught of it, Cricket," I mumbled. "I learned to reglaze a window when I was in cotts—"

Her hazel eyes burned with the warm smile. She was looking at my hands. Cricket was quite a small girl, no more than five feet in height. She had a rounded slenderness that gives a deceptively fragile appearance.

She also had very small, peculiar hands, and that made me think of a poem I'd just read, which in turn made my diaphragm lurch with a moan that might have been a sob.

Cricket's oval face was faintly pink, salted with pale freckles. Her nose just missed being upturned, her violet eyes just missed being too large, and her honey hair just missed being ruly, but in no respect did she miss being the most beautiful girl I have ever seen in all my strange life.

She left the doorway slowly and came into the room. For perhaps a minute, neither of us spoke—just stood there staring at each other while I tried to keep my face every bit as blank as hers. Clearly, this doll was carrying a chip on either porcelain shoulder. Looked like she'd ran over here in the middle of something else.

I wanted to knock both those chips off with my nose and not stop there. I'd never been with a girl, thinking the consequences perhaps a bit too electric and really just waiting for the right time. I was eighteen. The time would find me. Some cunning neural cell far within my head got up and wrote on the chalkboard for all the others that it had.

"I just want to know one thing." I grinned at my old classmate and set about filling in the gaps in my hypothesis. Dead silence spun out in the smoke from my new Tareyton. "What's your major?"

That freckled button nose began sending radar signals at the toes of her saddle Oxfords. "Double," she mumbled. "Art and astronomy. Although I was"—her head swiveled up, the blush not quite gone—"I was out on the quad. Professor Rhodes was a chemical engineer in the military, and he makes us read that Willy Ley and Hermann Oberth and—"

Then she recognized me, an act which to her should not have been rocket science.

"I . . . I remember you." She looked away. "Even before the bank robbery thing. That was in the *Sentinel*. You're the Connelly kid. What'd you go for, criminal justice?"

I closed the book I'd been reading, showed her the spine, *Uses of Discretion in Public Safety*, and made a face. "Yeah. Fucking freshman level. I think criminal justice is designed to weed out everyone but the true bastards."

I glanced at the shattered pane of lead glass. "Never, never forgot yeh from school." My face was burning. "No one like yeh."

She offered one black-gloved hand, "Once more, Connelly, I am so sorry—"

I had to not laugh. "Ummm, you owe Proctor Beaumont a fiver for that window. However . . ."

One second there was nothing, you see, and the next, Cricket Anne Bennigan was the center of my universe.

I stroked my chin with a rail of umbrella fingers. The tiny, overcoated blonde in the doorway still had no idea where to begin, nor did she look like she much wanted one. There would be time, there would be time, for introductions and ructions that a year would not reverse.

"If you were to bag class for the day, as I myself have undertaken, and join me at the Campus Grill for a few pitchers of Sung Kwok's finest pale ale, I would consider the matter all but resolved and eat the cost of your, uhh, space-exploration program . . ."

Cricket nearly fell on the floor laughing. "Um. Yeah. Okay. Yeah." The laughter faded quickly, but that furnace of warmth in her bright eyes didn't. "I don't know anybody here. I'm glad it was you."

"And no Brother Dom." I stood, hunting for tape and cardboard. I'd let the proctor know. When I felt like it. I screeched out an old folding chair for her to sit. She smelled like jasmine, I thought, and vanilla, and she was sitting *close*. "I got the first round."

I puffed up.

"You're trying to get me drunk. I'm really not that kind of girl." She punched me on the arm playfully, like Lo used to, and waited to see my reaction. "If that isn't the most convoluted pick-up line."

"Oh, I've got more," I began. "Have youse got a dime then? Ma' said to call the first time I ever fell in love. Or there was one I heard from my pal Jimmy Hennessy, he . . ."

Just then, Cricket burst out crying. No, really. Even we more-reconstructed Irish males are somewhat less than equipped at such times. In the moment, I scratched my head, handed her a clean handkerchief, and simply got up and held her until my starched white Sears and Roebuck shirt was gummy with girl-tears.

"Bad day at the office, dear?" I whispered. Cricket looked at my hands again and up into my eyes and shook her head sadly. Then she looked down and away. That look said I didn't need to know something or part of something. You get to know that look when it points down and away in that direction that quickly.

"Just broke off a bad, bad fling. I . . . got slapped around a few times. You can . . . this is okay, this is aces, but just be my friend, okay, until—"

"Hold on. Back up. Yer a bit ahead. I just want to go and get pissed, just yet, although we can certainly *talk*. You're . . ." My face was *flaming. Scarlet.* "Yer still cute as a warm kitten, yeh are."

Cricket smirked. "And you're still full of shit." That made me laugh, but . . . again, I'm Irish. I can only dim that switch so long. "He hit you, you say? Where's the wee naff live? I'll go fook 'im right out now. What's his name?"

I have never understood the look that Cricket gave me in return. "The East Village. I was at Columbia and just transferred here. I'm not staying anywhere that I get hit. His name's Caroline."

Full Stop.

"First pitcher's on me. Also the second." Then I watched her resume breathing. It was two pitchers to the dregs, and both of us talked so much we barely took a breath in between.

Then Cricket suggested we go walking. For the next five sodding *hours* with Cricket trying not to step on the earthworms and my own self trying not to touch her at all until the storm abated a bit if I could help it.

But right when I walked her to her door and we had to stop walking . . . I kissed her hand. It shocked her a little, I think, but she had her game-face on her.

"*Somewhere I have never traveled,*" I quoted that poem I saw that hurt my soul, something in some small-time magazine at the library, "*gladly beyond any experience. Your eyes have their silence. In your most frail gesture are things which enclose me or things I cannot touch because they are too near . . ."*

In Cricket's fabulous, smoky-amber eyes, something turned over and began to glow. It was something that would make me try to jump up and click my heels several times on the way back to men's halls, but every time it just looked like some sort of spastic trying to clap his big monkey feet together, so I knocked it off before anyone noticed, but that was a few minutes later. I meant to do it. I did.

"Edward Estlin Cummings." Cricket named off the poet smartly like she knew him.

"Aye," I answered. "He writes like his Shift key is broken."

She smiled at that, really smiled. Like I could make her really smile. "From *The New Yorker. Nobody, not even the rain, has such small h . . . h . . .*"

Cricket couldn't finish the citation but knew better than to try with words. When our lips touched, a blue spark happened behind my own eyes. "I wanted to do this ever since science class." she murmured, linking her hands behind my neck, looking into my eyes.

And that, as Pap-Pap would say, was simply that.

FEBRUARY 14, 1948: THE EXQUISITE CORPSE

Under Mari-huana with CB. This is SO much more fun than being drunk.

CB sat naked for four hours in this chilly dorm with the Visqueen over the damn rocket hole in the window, so I could draw her curves. We wrote for a while too after we got stoned. This is what we got:

When you throw something in storage, it never goes away. You come back to the attic to find everything moved about, holes in the floor, parts gone, parts rebuilt, parts blasted black through the roof.

Someday, all this will be yours unless you act now. Dullness is forced down a glittering blade, once razor-edged, now rusting in the mud of a receded seabed where among the dead a single ancestor forced her fins into a crawl, turning away from those she promised, kin she could have saved somehow?

That was just a dream. Wake into the same dead traces, straining up from chemical-cured science-project coal, the iridescent crystals growing to mock that which you're convinced you believe.

Amazing who looks like a freak. Amazing who looks sane and who looks nuts. The Crooked Man's house has roots much farther than we would suppose.

Sleeping in a graveyard, down by the highway.
The tunnels go farther back. Our future underground
is here already. Each burial marker, tomb wall, mound,
falling apart like a gingerbread house that got wet . . .

Nothing. Is personal. Is. Nothing. Must
become all that you fear. At times too scared
of what might crawl up from that subterrene
lower forty. The scene
changes
to flight:

Open your eyes, child,
out on the swamp, that poisoned
primordial stew, that wastewater-

graveyard. Getting there is all.
Do not despair.

Crawl up onto
the bank. Move on.
The water is clear.

Life
continues
in

despite . . .

Now in the studio where we sometimes sleep (when no one will be by next morn), I can smell wet wax and the hot promise of the cigarette groove in Cricket's lower lip, the honey of ancient plaster, the cold white room, the open skylight, the rain coming down outside while we make ferocious, barking love and scare the pigeons half to death. (The gargoyles don't mind.)

We can be all right now. The child inside may come forward. It is a far finer thing to be hunted and haggard and hollow of eye, eating from cans, watching crystal rain hiss down from sun-filled skies, that essential New York craziness I bring home from working up there on the weekends, talking to the artists and the crazy drunks in the Bowery, like that Joe Gould guy . . .

(here a line is struck out—CB)

New York, the descent farther back into older and older rooms, deeper layers of the Apple, farther down the ladder as the public eye closes more and more unto it, and the outside world sleeps through what goes on back here.

I suppose I'd better explain how I came to know New York more and more, specifically a little second-floor walkup on Broadway in the boro of Manhattan, just kitty-corner from the Biograph Theatre where the feds gunned down the outlaw John Dillinger.

It began with the sun on Cricket Bennigan's freckled skin that one day. Bennigan, begin again, alive in thine own skin again for the first time I'd seen all semester. One weekend with Cricket when we piled into the Hornet and bombed up there, up the hot, green, cowshit Miracle Mile of the turnpike.

The sun made Cricket glow from within, and I was reduced to idiocy at the sight, the sense, the mythic heat of her. When we stopped at a rest stop to sit in the sun, turning it into a picnic, my dear pixie let me rub lotion on her back and then put it on my face and wrists, clucking at my poor heat-trap gloves.

"We'll take a dip in the pool at the student union on the way back," Cricket suggested, gazing up at me in the rose-quartz sun where we were parked off the turnout. She was lying on a furry beach towel on the grass that was kept by FDR and John Q. Taxpayer.

I frowned. "Isn't it closed?"

Cricket's wicked grin made her look like a small, feral cat. "So?"

"It's the very devil yeh are, yeh caution," I said, and then she was trying to pin my wrists back, and I had my face in her neck, and on it went that day.

And on until we found Vizinczey's Rare Books, deep in the Bowery on a lower floor, looking out on an alley that had no name. Cricket oohed and aahed over first-edition copies of Charles Fort's scientifiction novel *The Outcast Manufacturers* and some reproduction editions of *Phantasmagoria* magazine—a local rag from last century that used to publish my very favorite mystery writer of all, Edgar Allan Poe. (I had to kiss her nose for that. Then I had to explain why.)

"I swear, you act just like—Connelly!" Cricket stamped her feet on the cold shop floor, breath smoking in the air under her complicated knit cap. My hands were warm in that year's incarnation of the gloves, but I'd looked longingly at the kerosene space heater by the cash register on the way in.

I wasn't looking there just then. Because the fat man was standing by like it was nothing, paging through a hidebound copy of Anthony Trollope, right in front of me. His wavy hair was going silver, his cheeks sunken, his sad eyes full of darkness.

He looked like a monster, an especially good person to have around in a crisis but a monster just the same. His nose was red from drink and something more. He was worn out and skited off. And I very nearly fell to my knees and crossed myself anyway.

Dashiell Hammett saw me looking, tried not to grin, and wagged a cautionary finger. "Keep on riding me, and they'll be picking iron out of your liver," he sidemouthed through the comprehensive smile.

Cricket waited, lost, for someone to explain the joke. I would in a moment. But these kinds of cars didn't pass me every day.

He waited. I knew this one. "The cheaper the crook, the gaudier the patter, eh?" One of the hinges on my knuckles squeaked involuntarily.

The greatest mystery writer I thought there was in the whole city, why, he looked at my gloves, scratched his balding pate and thought a moment, weaving the situation before him in with the joke he'd been about to make.

"I . . . I got nothin', kid. You know me. I don't know you."

"Shamus Connelly, Pinkerton Agency. This is my lucky Cricket. Cricket, this is Mister Dashiell Hammett, the fella who—"

Cricket shook his hand once, politely disinterested. "I saw *The Maltese Falcon*. It was okay. Kind of hard to follow though."

The beetling creatures that were Hammett's eyebrows furrowed upward for a moment. "I thought so too," he admitted. "Like they edited it too closely together. I did the screenplay, but I wasn't out on the cutting-room floor, oh no. Me and el señor director, well . . ."

He shook himself. "Best not to tell tales this far from school. You in school?"

I nodded. Hammett seemed to expect that. "Gah, wish I was spitting distance of your age. Can I buy you two nutty lovebirds lunch at Horn & Hardart's? Or a beer?" He sighed, "I could use a concert recital from the sweet bird of youth. I'm getting too old for my own research. Trying to actually *run* my own detective agency up here for the new book. You're in my racket, kid. You know they eat you alive on the overhead. They—"

And on. As we exited the bookstore, Hammett absentmindedly placed the book he'd been reading on a random shelf, just before the store dick started to get interested. And he talked. Oh, how he always talked.

I heard and processed everything the man said, but I had to talk too. I was a detective too, and it was time to sing like a little boid. I heard my own voice echoing from full fathom five, from Proxima Centauri, from half a dimension away between Dream and Wake.

"Would you have a job goin' then, Mister Hammett, for an old, seasoned guard such as myself?"

Hammett stopped where he was, stroked his mustache, and groaned. "I can't do that to your boss, kid. He probably needs men. He—"

I held up my hands. "They gave me a golden handshake on the way out the door. I stopped an armed robbery. We both ran out of ammo, and I choked the fella cold. It's in the report."

Cricket was looking at me with open awe. Hammett squinted blearily, trying to remember something. "You think you could get WPA money or whatever they call it now, like a . . . whatchamacallit, like an independent study?"

I bit my lip. "I think thirty dollars a week plus expenses, and I'll bring yer coffee."

He chuckled. "Kid, we'll talk. I'm a bonded officer, and I know a cute little number who works over in the registrar's office at Columbia U. She can dope out what forms we need and how much long green this is gonna take to put on wheels. Now let's all go have a drink on it." When we shook hands, I made his comb-over stand on end and show his bald spot.

OLD GHOSTS WITH BIG GUNS

June 19, 1950

But this, too, passed. Funny how time speeds up the older you get. You'd think it would be the other way around.

Funny how even the greatest things in life fall through in the end. The truest lover dies and leaves you, or you die and leave them. I had no idea what to expect. I guess that's good. It is now.

It is now. But then, it looked more like:

I hate my boss. Hate. Hate. Hate my boss. Knew this was too good to be true. Hammett was only ever a good writer, not anything else, and he should never be in the slightest bit involved with any business that involves *people*—

Working for his new Continental Detective Agency in Manhattan a few weeks out of the month (he was running it as kind of a real-world research project for a new book or movie or some such thing, I never quite got that clear) was an offer I couldn't refuse.

Sure, it looked good on a resume, but Dashiell Hammett of all people had me staking out divorcées and divorcés on back-to-back shifts, sometimes twelve hours at a time on country roads in the Hudson, peeing in the woods and waiting to go home to gick in a proper toilet like a proper human being. After a while, it got dodgy.

"My Da' didn't bring the union to Callaight County so I could sit here and . . ." the argument always began.

"Why, you mouthy little Mick. You think you wanna work anywhere in this town again?" That was good. That meant the argument would end well. It was when Hammett started *not* talking that I got worried.

When he talked, you see, when he gave you shite, you were supposed to give it back to him. Then he was your best mate for life and all on about this and that, what was happening with his family . . .

I remember the Fong Chong Teahouse on Mott Street in Manhattan. In the back, the old dragon who founded it during the early part of the century is buried in an urn of ashes in the foundation. Cool, stuffy air blows out from the smoky cave.

Dashiell Hammett has been coming here for weeks, trying to dope out a straight answer, concerning something called *The Titan Bible* for a "big fat paycheck of an account" he just got "down your way," meaning my hometown. Powersburg, nowhere fookin' PA. Dashiell won't say from where, who, or what. This is for senior staff, he tells me, admitting nothing.

But the name on the check stub I saw last night was Ross Ehrend IV, when I did his books behind his back. Curiouser and curiouser. I saw a name that meant nothing underneath—

Subject of Surveillance: August Derleth.

But the parentheses made me whistle.

(Executor: Effects and Writings of Dcdnt. Howard Phillips Lovecraft.)

"So lemme . . ." Just now, Hammett is wobbly. The top two buttons on his Hawaiian shirt are undone. His face is very red. He looks like a jolly tomato.

I giggle, high on the tea. This is the best independent study ever, when I can play the mad cunt out a bit, and the scary thing is that we're doing *research*. Or were anyway before I spilled the proverbial beans.

"Lemme get this straight . . . you can build up and hold a static charge in your forearms and kinda throw it through your"—he loosens a tie that isn't there—"hands there at somethin' that'll take it in, or it just . . . *dissipates*?"

I sway over my bottle of Yuengling lager, best-kept secret of my part of the world that Hammett has never had before tonight.

The beer and smoking all those left-handed cigarettes make all the neon outside look warm, every language, Mandarin, Cantonese, Mexican Spanish, Puerto Rican bodega-creole, and everything in between. All of Times Square is a penny arcade to me now, and all the junkies, wide-eyed girls, and bitter old men and traffic cops merely players.

"Pretty much. Think of it like dowsing for wells or some such bollocks. I don't pretend to understand it. I've no explanation for it. It's just . . ." I try to grin. I must look like a melon. "Just a trick I learned."

I'm trying to speak Hammett's language, but the city is just too beautiful when I'm this high. Just too damn much. I wipe my eyes behind the optician-tweaked welding goggles and shoehorn myself into the moment.

I'm telling my best-kept secret to my hero, whom I now despise when I see him out behind the page. "You're high," the great detective informs me. "You're fucking higher than shit. You're funny when you're high, Irish. You should sell that one to John W. Campbell at *Astounding*! Anyway, your round, squirt. Mine's the lager again . . ."

My interests are elsewhere now, and the myth is never like the man.

Then one cold Friday afternoon not long later, when there was still a dusting of snow getting in my collar through the badly tied black scarf, I rushed down to work, still bleeding from a round with the razor, and stayed in the Hornet, letting her idle at the curb.

I knew nothing. I was still nothing but Hammett's hired help. Remember that well, stranger, as ye pass by and look on me now, choked by a black shroud of decades behind the locked green door of 722 Marlon Street—or as I call it now, square one.

Remember that now. I knew nothing. This is all that happened when they got me.

This is all. I am no junkie fiending for a hit, but a sane man fighting for his soul. A bit longer, I beg your indulgence, and absolutely nothing shall become clear. But you shall see.

When I tried and squinted down my glasses, I could read the bold type of the newspaper article someone had pasted to the chain-locked door of the Continental Detective Agency, a stinky, old former gymnasium, floor-waxed into recalcitrant submission as an office building, a long wing of a place full of fans and cigar butts and hooers coming around looking for a hand-out.

"Author Hammett Blackballed as Communist; Closes Local Detective Agency."

I groaned. The masthead was unmistakably *The New York Times*.

On the Hudson's seat in front of me was the plum lead I'd gotten the night before and taken home. My first real case. It wasn't from a private citizen but a civil body. And not the goddamn Civil Rights Congress either.

No matter what that Joe McCarthy said, I never saw that side of Dash. Ever. Yes, I know he went to meetings, but it was after the close of business. No, we never kept anything about it in the office that I saw. No, I . . .

I didn't get called before Senator Torquemada's dog-and-pony revue down in

Washington. I got a few telephone calls, and one time some men came to both our dormitory halls.

I wasn't there. They said they knew me from school, but Cricket said she never knew any of them at Our Lady of the Alleghenies. Not a one. Sections of the bale of paperwork from the Pennsylvania state attorney general's office screamed up from the page, off the record and independently contracted, of course, to send in the expendable to do the unnecessary for the ungrateful, except maybe, maybe . . .

. . . first of several investigations into financial deviations and patient torture going far beyond the Geneva Convention, even beyond the original Pennsylvania System of Confinement used by the Quakers during commonwealth times. The actions of these individuals operating within government will be determined possibly hazardous to national security, including even radiation tested on VA patients without their informed consent.

President Truman stated, "I believe rigid, strict confinement of people with diseases they did not choose to catch, that such a thing is cruel and wrong. We must let the facts speak for themselves.

Interpol warns that individuals operating within the federal government may be aiding and abetting known war criminals Martin Bormann and Dr. Joseph "Angel of Death" Mengele for purposes of crimes against humanity.

If approached by anyone from the McCarthy commission, licit or illicit, the following telephone numbers should be called immediately. There is immunity of a limited nature here and may be sufficient.

The Hornet's shotgun door *kerchunked* open and shut. Shamus screamed and nearly pulled leather, spilling reams of paper across the seat and the floorboards. Cricket's hands in their gray velvet gloves stayed his own for a moment.

"I took the goddamned train up here. They're tearing both our dorms to bits back at school," she told him bluntly. "Drive."

Cricket saw the look and answered it. "I don't *know* where! To downtown Powersburg. They won't dare try anything down by the cop-shop. Reed knows you, or whatever that Chief's name is. Just someplace until this blows over. Drive."

As the pedal hit the floor, Cricket slammed the door on her side shut a second time. The guy up the street who'd started to walk toward them turned away and said something into his sleeve.

Shamus and Cricket drove for hours through dark streets and across darker lots with Junior Walker on the radio, and Howlin' Wolf and Les Paul. Shamus could read Cricket Bennigan's mind more than intuitively. She pleaded with the small white face of a lonely, frightened child.

Shamus felt shame in himself, as if there was something inside of him waiting for something. An asthmatic clock somewhere was striking ten. He lit a cigarette for each of them. "I reckon I'm getting to be an old maid, but I've had all I want tonight."

Cricket said nothing, just looked at his true knuckles inside the gloves, all of them presumably white where they were locked on the steering wheel. Was there no end to this piling of mystery upon violence? He had the sensation of being caught in a monstrous net whose meshes were slimy with something silver he didn't want to know about, something he thought of every time he washed his hands.

"What's the game? And if we're going to be brought in, what's it all about? What started it? This?" He threw the folder into the backseat. Cricket watched it land.

"Don't ask me," she said, looking tired and old all of a sudden. "I just got here. I've had it up to here with all this weird crap they have you do for no money, chasing all these fake census records and where the money goes, who it pays to kill and who to keep alive . . . who CARES?!?"

When Cricket raised her voice, he nearly wrecked into an old panel truck whose driver honked at him and said a few discouraging words in colorful Bronx vernacular.

"What a killing!" Shamus thumped the satchel of files on the backseat to his left. "They're hoarding their little orgy of evidence plus a lot more up at that old state hospital, and *they're gonna burn it to the ground next month, or whatever they're tryin' to figure out now, it says there! It—*"

Cricket looked like she wanted to bite his throat out. Her violet eyes were full of weary incomprehension, the patience gone from any look. "Who's *they*?" she asked. "I thought you were just taking motel pictures . . ."

"Don't make me turn this car around . . ." Shamus sighed. "They're too suspicious as it is for us to linger much longer. But things are about ripe for the fire that's to start in the nut ward and spread to the whole hospital. Hundreds of bodies found in the ruins. Never was there a sweeter con."

For that, his true love had no ready answer. *Motel pictures . . . I am too good at hiding my tracks.*

Shamus cut across two lanes of traffic. Then they were over the TriBorough Bridge, she was pretty sure, headed into Jersey with another rhythm-and-blues station on the radio, some new cat calling himself Brother Ray. The seats smelled like tobacco and boys: good smells, smells she loved.

Cricket closed her eyes, knowing that she could never sleep again in her strange life. When she opened them, they were back at school. Shamus whirled away from the gate, leaped through flowerbeds, crossed the porch in a bound, and was in the dorm. Behind him, Cricket's feet clattered.

"SHAMUS JOSEPH CONNELLY ARE YOU OUT OF YOUR MOTHERFUCKING MIND?!? WHAT IN THE HELL—"

But no answer came as they ran through an empty hallway, an empty room, another. Nobody was in sight on the ground floor of the men's hall. Shamus went up to door #106, his, which was ajar. The room was full of light.

Shamus's face lost all serenity as he saw inside.

"Here I was worried about going and getting my gun."

Cricket started backing up. Fast. A madrigal choir sang in her blood. Something was so very, very wrong. There was a muffled shattering of glass, an explosion, and the sharp whine of a bullet past his ear.

He'd been fired at through the big feng shui mirror in the front hall, the multifaceted one Tien had arranged for the convenience of those he called "the unseen guests." A second shot

rang
and
time
stood
still.

A cool wind blew breath across the mirror, across the back of his neck, making the fine blonde-red hairs stand. Rooted into that hard, knobby thing going up and down the middle of his back, the one he sometimes remembered he owned, was fully in possession of, and even—may the saints preserve us— that he occasionally knew how to use.

Before the bullet was silent, it seemed, Shamus had shot out a hand. Something happened to both his shoulders: a twist and . . . caught himself. By some miracle of the gods, the hat stayed on.

And Shamus Connelly blew the bullet backward with the charge from his hands, from the weird shimmer around his arm that fell like a marble column with a cuff link, from his flipper hand turning cold, the veins turning purple, the fillings screaming, screaming, oh SCREAMING in his teeth, and the buckle on his belt making an imprint in his skin, ow, ow owwwowwowwwowowww . . .

But he never made a noise. He never flinched. That wasn't in his job description. His face, though, was nothing anyone ever wanted to see awake or asleep. Under his hat, his short red hair was standing on end. "Want to try that again?" he growled in a brogue that nearly needed subtitles.

Then he realized that he'd fired himself dry.

"You were right the first time, Tally. This existence is empty for you," the Man with No Face said as he slithered out, calling his red-capped, flak-vested dogs off from behind him. "Bennigan, you're not worth my time. Not enough meat. Dump you out on Loop Road. Connelly . . ."

He surveyed Shamus. "What, you think you get to be a *hero*? You think you get a *life*? I *let* you live, Taliesn. So I could hunt you down, reincarnation after reincarnation, and strip your ego *bare*. Every time. Welcome to hell."

(*Nonononono.*)

The lightning drowned him out. But in the end, they took them down.

[FINALE]

ANGEL OF DEATH

DEMAREST STATE HOSPITAL FOR THE CRIMINALLY INSANE
POWERSBURG, PENNSYLVANIA
ARBEIT MACHT FREI

"Let the avenue to this house be rendered difficult and gloomy by mountains and morasses. Let the doors be of iron, and let the gratings, occasioned by opening and shutting them, be increased by an echo that shall deeply pierce the soul."
—Dr. Benjamin Rush, 1787

"In the beginning was the Worm. In the Worm was the Mess, and the perception of the Mess, into degrees of Light and Shadow, Chord and Discord. When things began to separate, Life began to hurt."
—Nostradamus, *Biblia Titanica*

10 November 1952

(I Think)

Now and then, my mind goes silent, dripping down these madhouse walls.

The entire structure is dank local granite, like a railroad bridge, like the jailhouse. There have been many murders and suicides in this institution. Some of their imprints follow you up the stairs and knock your hat off your head.

General Washington once remarked that, "Though admirable enough in means, the place entire feels not unlike some stagnant castle of the Old World with all its many oubliettes, dungeon keeps, and boots and racks." The great political scientist Alexis de Tocqueville marveled, "In this new country, it seems the keeping of the mad is done, as all else, on a mob scale by conscripted louts." Nothing changes but the year.

Demarest Hospital is a tall, foreboding black pipe organ, a Dracula's castle of an unfinished prison with iron gates and stone battlements, converted into a sanitorium indicative of what awaits the being who enters. "He who made me was moved by eternal justice," reads the plaque over the door. "I was created with all eternal things, ergo I endure forever."

Many who passed through those grieving gates knew the next line of Dante's *Inferno* by heart and said the bastard English version aloud. "Abandon all hope, ye who enter here." But the inscription in Allegheny granite below it, laboriously chiseled, was German, not Italian. The Boss had it commissioned special. "A R B E I T M A C H T F R E I." Where few can see.

I cannot tell this story the way I so desperately want to, or I fear my head should burst. Suffice to say that I have learned one thing. We are the mirror, and the Dreamwalk—the world between worlds—is but the reflection. This life is the dream.

I must humble myself. I must offer up all this suffering to myself, say yes to myself, and disappear up my own bum like the man in the Bosch painting. There. I'm laughing. Even smashed on the rocks of time in this madhouse, they can't . . . they can't get that.

This journal is very small, twisted up and stuffed in the wall in hope I ever get out of here, in hope the hell-fiend Mengele will let me squeak with something besides the voluntary surrender of my poor hands that have been through so much already.

This room has insulated walls. They cuff my hands in rubber flex. They took me by surprise, and Superman doesn't seem to be showing up.

Dr. Mengele won't let me leave until I let them chop off my hands for "study and display," the old Kraut had the gall to say into my face. I hear he once sewed two twins together to make Siamese twins. I hear his collection of dead freaks rivals that of the Philadelphia College of Surgeons. I hear he is working on perfecting some sort of organic pain transmitter.

I hear. With frequent upward glances, the Angel of Death assures himself you are still paying attention. He talks louder than the closh and clack and clang of the work that goes on in here, louder than the screams and the other sounds that are so much worse and last so much longer on the wards.

In my cell, one ray of light focuses hot on one point of the asbestos tile. I say as little as possible when company comes. "Das ist aber Schäde," I once mouthed off to Mengele in high-school German, higher than the twelve courts of high on the drugs they whack me up with in here, that Thorazine, not knowing what the hell I was saying. "Ich—"

But I got no further before Uncle Azrael backhanded me. It hurt. "Do not pollute the new Reich by speaking German to me!" he shrieked. "I have no time for the pablum you are fed. I have experiments to get on with. Our leader is doing just fine. He's"—he cleared his throat—"just not anywhere you can reach him at the moment. Now if you would please hold still . . ."

High out of my skull, I looked into Mengele's mind and saw a vacant-eyed child, doodling tracks in the dust with a spare dissecting-pin in his idle hand, the working hand vivisecting just . . . so . . .

I saw delight in the struggle of the animal model, the stiff rigor of slave flesh resisting, the pulsing organs on cheap display.

I saw the part where he ran. The Germans would have hung him and set him on fire. The Russians would have eaten him or worse.

But certain elements within the OSS made him an offer, a cover of farm labor and hiding out with the Argentines, for working on Project Paperclip for something called an unknown investor under something called a black budget.

"Little railroad town in Pennsylvania, doc," the bored operative told him. "Boss said to tell you there's okay skiing close by." No Odessa, although a certain official at the Vatican figured very prominently in the paperwork.

The Angel of Death studied the original plans, intrigued by the concept of "changing the behavior of inmates through confinement in solitude with labor." Demarest had been refurbished in the twenties, he read, to relieve scandalous overcrowding conditions at Locke Mountain and Torrance Hospital.

The radiation tests from the Atomic Energy Commission would more than pay for everything. Everything. All Mengele's research . . . all . . . his research . . . would receive funding the likes of which the Reich could never have put up. It was a glorious time, more than worth the wound he took in the ballocks with a hot iron that made him unfit for service.

It was Mengele who reinstituted the old Pennsylvania System of confinement at Demarest as a basic work protocol in the first place. Inmates were not allowed to communicate in any way or meet for any purpose, including religious services. Ministers of various denominations preached their homilies whilst walking up and down the halls.

No one was allowed to make music of any kind, including with human tongue, or see anything having to do with the outside world. Each cell had its own ten-by-fourteen exercise yard, which inmates were allowed in for one hour a day.

However, Mengele's own wrinkle was to test experimental drugs for the Office of Strategic Services, and for private pharmaceutical manufacturers, on every single inmate. This made manageability much more cost-effective and eliminated the need for the "diving-bell" or cage-type helmets formerly worn by the handlers and orderlies on top of the kind of padded gloves, normally used to train attack dogs, and other gear more commonly worn behind the plate by the catcher in baseball.

Tunnels weren't unusual at Demarest. In fact, they were the favored means of escape. Renovations in the 1930s uncovered an estimated thirty incomplete inmate-dug tunnels. But upon further local independent study in the area of cryptozoology, it was rumored, Mengele found a way around that with the introduction of certain native species of predatory amphibian into the water pipes at key junctions . . .

The Angel of Death stood on the tarmac of Sinking Springs airfield in the memory I saw, glossy heels clicking together. One of those heels was worn differently than the other, held in place with bolts.

"I like the way the wind sits here, on the tongue," Josef mused to himself, breath fragrant with schnapps. "I could work here. Günther, my bags . . ."

The air was foul, but Mengele seemed to thrive on it, even on the smell of shit and methane gas from the low-balled Army Corps of Engineers plumbing job and the faint breath of kerosene and coal that was the Demarest excuse for heat.

There were already chain mounts in the walls and places outside where individuals could be waterboarded. It was as if some benevolent St. Nicholas had designed him an amusement park.

If this was hell, Josef chose to reign. As it had been at Auschwitz-Birkenau, those inmates who were physically and mentally capable of menial labor were expected to work, and those who had no skill were trained in one.

Thus did this strange government sanitarium recoup its own million-plus-dollar price tag and the flak they were taking from the Limeys about the use of solitary confinement and sensory deprivation. If you weren't insane when you went in, the *London Times* famously reported, you would be when you left.

Every screw that ever walked a turn at Demarest would swear on a stack of bibles that solitary confinement was good for the soul for those people who had driven themselves insane by excessive masturbation or impious living. Though apparently well on admission, the refrain ran, many of those types are strongly predisposed to mania.

Then, just at that point, Josef Mengele clouded his mind to me and clouded mine. That truly hurt. It's been some time. I can't . . . think right all the time now. Not all the time.

I live in the Dream now most of the time until they wake me up. But I can't find Cricket. She won't talk to me.

What are my struggles compared to the very heaps of bones that make every street in this county? Archives of unsolved kidnappings and murders remain open on the books of the Powersburg police.

Everything is just grist for the mill, bricks for the wall, and not a one of those bastards has any interest in preventing crime, merely *directing* it . . . I don't know which branch of the government these Project Paperclip fucks report to. I don't know if they do either.

But I know who brought me here and that all along the Dream was the real life. I was really Tally, and he was really me. Was. Really. Me.

Triggered again. That's what the fucking fake shrink calls it. I close my eyes for a moment to shut out the snowblind stone white of the walls . . .

Strange lights like paper lanterns hover at the edges of my vision, and there's a certain humming in my ears, and I am out and away, floating through nightmare town like a little child's lost balloon.

Through the Dreamwalk, watching grim-eyed fire brigade in leather plague suits filtering behind the scenes of rooftop dream-speakeasies like the inevitable Keystone Cops banging on everyone's perceptual doors from somewhere outside, come round through the grinding, hungover dawn to seed the ground with salt.

I can't stay in the Dream. Here and now is too beautiful and weird, sitting at my window. Merciful cloudbanks shroud the wasteland with shadows.

Hungry railroad ghosts reel in the eaves and fill the streets, the rotting rooftops, power lines, phone lines, and every other line of bullshit Thomas

Edison foisted off on America, jackal bastards tearing down the quietly extraordinary in favor of the loudly boring and easily disposable, building after building, freeway after freeway, city after Potemkin village mockup made to be smashed flat by what rough beast on camera as the top one percent watch from a lead-lined bunker somewhere far away and munch popcorn like ants on a corpse.

I can't stop doodling in the margins, ha ha. Thought I had it so bad when I could still use my hands, before they pumped them full of Demerol every morning and tied them tight.

They don't really care what I write down. No one will ever, ever see it. I've written it all. Drawn it all, the old, crowded walls with high-arched ceilings and little weird church skylights, the food hole and peephole in every door.

Someone is always watching here on the borderland of this new "Cold War." You learn to believe in God and pray for salvation else ye shall surely go mad.

No one knows how I happened, merely the product of a creator who threw in horrifying abilities to counteract horrifying disabilities. The nodules in me contain, by definition, massive amounts of silicate dust.

Silicosis. What caused black lung in Pap-Pap made me the son a partially silicon-based critter to whom one or two different statutes of the physical laws apply. Ah?

But my peers and contemporaries do not follow Planck and de Broglie and Einstein, you mind. All they cared to know when I was small was that their little flipper baby could draw down the lightning.

Sunday Shaw at the *Sentinel* was going to bankroll Hammett's contract for me to go deep cover into Demarest State Hospital as a patient and investigate the whole system. That's what that file folder Cricket saw was all about.

They railroaded me here first. Ha. Ha. Hahahaha. My cover got blown before I even got to read through the whole thing. As that fucking duck in the cartoons would say, it is to laugh. But it doesn't even matter now.

They're engineering the very end of the world here, straight up to that *thing* that was never human, the one who really signs all the paychecks, he . . .

What is the measure of the human soul under standard conditions? Got to breathe. I don't even remember how long I've been here, so what the hell am I even on about?

The hall is empty now. I'm taking this notebook with me, pausing every few feet to record this wonderment with my right hand. I'm dreaming this. They got my hands. They. My. Got. They.

Hands. The hall has always been empty. Ever since my door was just open. And I could just walk out into the hall. With no hands. But got. Feet. Feet can. Walk. Walk.

Walk. Sing swing the sickening bells of Bedlam. Means have not justified terrible end.

Got up and left, and the door was still open, but I cannot punish. The fathers have sinned and looted and left, absconded with my hands.

With my hands. I need a hand. Give me a hand. I. Hand.

They took my hands. Every building is crumbling here in the Dreamwalk version of the asylum. Trees grow through the roofs of many floors.

The doors are too small for me to get through because I outgrew them, and I could stay here, but I'd be living in garbage three layers deep and shit and bugs that camp in your hair.

Every piece of metal on the property seems to be rusting, every piece of plaster crumbling at one time. Demarest was originally administered by Quaker reformers who believed in penitentiary punishment with a design taken from Jeremy Bentham's famous panopticon back in merrie old England.

Each cellblock was to radiate in different directions from the hub. This allowed easy view of every block from the center, and the way in was through three giant sets of double-locking doors. Upon coming through all three sets of doors, inmates were generally fitted with black hoods, which they would wear at all times—

Then the Dream rips open and carries me away from the hospital kingdom of the dead and its mad monarch drawing near, surgeon of the noblest blood, surgeon of demise without mercy, *Head of Surgery, meaning of pain and the showers of slow decay, and yes, this just went on over in Germany just a little*

while ago, and yes, we wiped it out, we did, we did, we, shhhhh, now let the
medication work . . .

He is always with me. I can always hear him talking, talking, talking. Der
Todtengel. The Angel of Death.

Sssshh . . . this is just the new prototype but shhh shhh even the Japs knew
about this . . . shhh shhh . . . the Japs have a facility three times this size on Na
Hale Moku out Hawaii way . . . yes, this is why we fought Pearl Harbor . . . but
it's all the same team now, us . . . and you.

We need to kill about a billion of you to get the population manageable, but you
didn't hear about that yet, and you won't remember this . . . and when you have
finished coughing out that pound of flesh and bone through your cored throat all
over their unloving hands, you will be rewired, wirebrushed, and cured to go forth
and sin no more. Good night . . . and may all your dreams be wonderful.

This is the locked lavatory they are using for an operating room, the start
of it all. "I have to interrupt myself," Dr. Mengele says. "I'm chattering. Here is
the instrument in its tripartite form. The steel table with its blood gutters. The
iron restraints. And of course the Stryker saw. Pay attention. This will count as
ninety percent of the final."

The sun is uncommonly strong. It beats down through the skylight and traps
me until I can hardly collect my thoughts. Mengele is adjusting screws on a
machine near to his hand with a cunning little electric screwdriver.

Mengele's eyes are as distant and dark as the empty sockets of a skull. "Did
you ever imagine that this was all just a bad dream from which you were nearly
ready to awaken?"

Behind us, the jailer-thing in his red cap winds my chain around both wrists
and leans on his carbine, letting his malformed head hang backward. He smells
like a tainted cheese. He is trying to follow what is to come. Some distant, non-
drugged part of me envies his ignorance.

My head is a cage full of dead rats. Mengele places a hollow iron shoehorn in
my mouth and forces me to bite down.

"Observe, how he has to let in the gag, otherwise the straps around the neck
would snap it here," he gestures. "We had total support all along, Shamus.
No one wants to admit it. I'm asking you. Should such a life's work come to
nothing? Should people let that happen? There's no time to lose. People are
already building a case against me. People are cowards."

Mengele's voice pins me back to the moment like a bug on a card. "Since you must know, weapons sales are unregulated and global. That includes, at the moment, biological weapons. We're trying to create race-specific plagues, you see. Streamline the whole overpopulation problem. It's my"—he permits himself a small chuckle—"modest proposal. Or was. To your Office of Strategic Services. It's why I'm *alive*, boy." He bends over, fiddling with something on the console. "Ah, hold still. Very good. Can you still build up a charge in the hands? Is there any feeling?"

A shudder crosses my skin. His grin is pestilential. "We're working on a virus over in Africa. Those missionaries never change the needles they use. Never mind." Mengele comes back into himself, realizing that he's still talking.

"The injustice of this process and the inhumanity of its execution are beyond doubt. At this point, I would ask if you remember how you got here?"

Nothing.

"You are Shamus Joseph Connelly of Powersburg, Pennsylvania, child of Joseph and Anna Connelly, and lately amorously inclined with a young lady of un-American proclivities . . . eine lesbisch . . . named Cricket Bennigan. Hmmp. Deputized by President Truman at Hoover's orders. Oh, we knew Hoover in the drag clubs in Berlin before the wall went up. Anyhow, yes, yes, you were Hoover's deputy. Sent in to investigate claims of . . . oh, it just gets funnier and funnier . . . Unknown radiation being tested on the inmates of this facility for the criminally insane! How dare we execute our decent American convicts before they're *ripe*? Let's send in a green fucking night watchman who can barely even hold a gun! I ask you. Why are you here? You are here because I want you here."

Mengele leers at my hands. In that leer, I feel more soiled than memory permits, which isn't much. "Not all of you. I throw a switch, the hands will live"—he gestures above and below the stocks at the smoked glass—"in these self-sealing bottles. Then the rest of you is free to go. I have no further need of your services—what is the American—gumshoe."

The words make little sense. But their frequency and variety seem to indicate that Dr. Mengele is asking my judgement. I shut my eyes and throw up all over the machine, rattling the brass rods at the front.

The machine is freshly cleaned and glows. In front of many eyes, my forearms are laid beneath the harrow. No discordant note disturbs the work of the machine. Many people do not look anymore at all.

Outside, merciful cloudbanks roll in. It will rage rain all night.

Clap. Clap. Clap. Mengele drops to one knee, fist to forehead in the odd kowtow of the Thule Society. A yellow, tapering hand strokes the doctor half-tenderly behind the ear. The green stone glimmers, muted in the light, from the scrolled silver setting on the ring finger.

"You are free."
The Man with No Face devours Josef Mengele piecemeal.
Willingly.

I awaken. I think. The clean, trembling smell of the spring afternoon with the beech trees outside, breaking into bud, almost negates that odd black membrane over the sunlight like always. The air is cool lead-crystal, pregnant, waiting.

Outside the window, two birds wheel overhead under the black storm clouds, throwing themselves at each other and always missing. As it was in the beginning, is now, and ever shall be.

The walls of this asylum are fifty feet high and ten feet thick. The legends within it are legion, frozen in dusty sunbeams where no birds sing in the walls or dance in the light.

Time is out of joint here. The clocks have melted down. The gods have all gone home.

Outside my window are gray glowing clouds and two white doves, side-by-side on the telephone wire. The wind sings through the pines on this unbelievable morning.

Out there is the back end of Short Mountain and the bowl of the valley where I used to fly kites on the opposite side, the Dysart side, back in the clean world. This is a side of town where I never had any reason to be for a long time.

And what was the angle, anyway? Since when do fucking military police ever guard a state hospital for criminal nutters? Three of them used to circle around the perimeter in a Jeep with orders to shoot anything that tried to run.

Yes, I said *anything*. I saw Ward Nine when they ran me in here. I'll tell you about that when these damn drugs wear off. If they ever do.

This has all got a bit beyond my experience. My face is still broken from that inbred orderly showing me who was boss. I can see light, and that's about all, just light and shadow, like Plato emerging from the cave.

I can't tell hands that feed from hands that hit. Everything I thought I knew has been buggered. Buggered. Nothing for it but to keep buggering on.

This is not how life was supposed to go. One has to wonder where it all went wrong. When I try to sleep at night, I feel them trying to slip a tag around my toe. In my mind, I see the table set and a hook-handed nonagenarian at my place, his old eyes canceled by the fog of junk.

In my mind, I see the autopsy table set and a shape under the sheet in my place, under the knife, the last page of me sprayed with blood on sterile walls.

But we don't discuss these things in this house. We don't talk about anything real. We prescribe away the sniffles and let tumors grow to human size. There is a bigger problem here that can strike anywhere, and none will know the hour when the master comes to call.

We are prisoners of our blood, which likes to lay waste. All we may hope to do is sing it to sleep for as long as possible. There is static on my line between sender and receiver, between signal and noise, a towering silhouette looming on my splattered wall, shifting in shape.

Shifting in shape. But now I can see his face. Now I can process. His face.

Always the same. An inhuman half-moon of a thing, a profile like a thumb and forefinger poised to pinch, impeding all my impetus, feeding on impotence, exploiting ignorance, making everyone an enemy.

I can't feel my hands anymore. I. Hand. Eye. Look, Ma, look

No hands.

But I can remember his face. The day is bloody. The day is gone. The dream is real. The blackbirds are rough.

(Faster, faster, fall the pages of the incredibly ornate flipbooks I used to make myself draw in the corners of my school hornbooks, a whole world shuttling out between crabbed black lines that seem to form words of a sort, signal behind flicker, motion, the illusion of depth . . .)

After all this time, the silence is the worst thing.

The silence that was the first thing I heard when I finally managed to drag myself back up those two flights of glassed-in stairs on my weeping stumps, screaming, "Then sings my soul, My Saaavior God, to Theee . . ."

And no one answered. There was just that nothing. That yellow-gray light outside like we were about to get a twister, the way we did every third summer in my back-alley shantytown, so the richies up on Heaven Hill Road could call us townies tornado-bait Irish one more time.

There's that score settled in my head at least. But not the zero-sum of climbing back to daylight from that solitary shithouse and seeing only offices stripped as bare as battlefield corpses.

I screamed and screamed and screamed, but there was not a damned soul to scream at until the FBI showed up, and then I screamed at them quite a bit, and someone gave me a shot.

And then I woke up in a home with a nice young tutor, who came three times a week and taught me a million and one uses for my Swiss Army hooks, as she called them. Amanda Thompson taught me a million things. But by then, it was 1959, and Mandy was in psych at Columbia for God's sake, traveling down across the border into the land of the ridge runners and stump-jumpers. *Of her own free will.*

My stumps itched, but it was already no strain to push a wheelchair as long as I didn't try to walk the motherfucker up to ninety. In any event, Mandy was literate and well-read enough to distract me from the pain of the PT and get me taking the Eukodal most of the time. She said it would wean me off the morphine. I have my doubts.

When I take morphine, the silence loses its power to kill me. Nothing comes then. No faerie takes, nor witch hath power to charm. No sick, misbegotten ghost can rob me of the chance . . .

To cast my soul outward, meditate into the next life. The next time I lay down this body, I want some kind of assurance from Mandelbrot . . . or his kind . . . that last time pays for all.

And if I don't get that, I'm going to hold my breath until I live forever. I've had enough.

I can lay down this body like an ant for the next re-spawn and let Connelly go on to better worlds than these. Wheelhorse and the rest of the old farts might have a few ideas. I see them in my dreams more as I get older. And for longer each time . . .

Still, it's going to be a long century . . .

§

Edward Morris has been nominated for the British Science Fiction Association Award, the Rhysling Award, and the Pushcart Prize In Literature. His short fiction has appeared over 150 times worldwide in markets from *Interzone* to *The Lovecraft Ezine*, *Perihelion SF*, and *Big Pulp*. Print anthologies include *The Children of Gla'Ki: Tribute Stories To Ramsey Campbell*, Ellen Datlow's *Best Horror of the Year*, *The Worlds of Philip Jose Farmer*, and *ReAnimators!* His short stories have been translated into Japanese, Italian, Finnish, Polish, Hungarian, and most recently, Egyptian Arabic with Dr. Ahmed Al-Turki's fantastic translation of "Jihad Over Innsmouth" from *The Book of Cthulhu*. Morris is a multiple sclerosis survivor who lives and works in Portland, Oregon, as an author and bouncer.

BROKEN EYE BOOKS

Sign up for our newsletter at
www.brokeneyebooks.com

Welcome to Broken Eye Books! Our goal is to bring you the weird and funky that you just can't get anywhere else. We want to create books that blend genres and break expectations. We want stories with fascinating characters and forward-thinking ideas. We want to keep exploring and celebrating the joy of storytelling.

If you want to help us and all the authors and artists that are part of our projects, please leave a review for this book! Every single review will help this title get noticed by someone who might not have seen it otherwise.

And stay tuned because we've got more coming . . .

OUR BOOKS

The Hole Behind Midnight, by Clinton J. Boomer
Crooked, by Richard Pett
Scourge of the Realm, by Erik Scott de Bie
Izanami's Choice, by Adam Heine
Pretty Marys All in a Row, by Gwendolyn Kiste
Queen of No Tomorrows, by Matt Maxwell
The Great Faerie Strike, by Spencer Ellsworth
Catfish Lullaby, by A.C. Wise
Busted Synapses, by Erica L. Satifka
Boneset & Feathers, by Gwendolyn Kiste
Alphabet of Lightning, by Edward Morris

COLLECTIONS
Royden Poole's Field Guide to the 25th Hour, by Clinton J. Boomer
Team Murderhobo: Assemble, by Clinton J. Boomer

Stay weird.
Read books.
Repeat.

brokeneyebooks.com
twitter.com/brokeneyebooks
facebook.com/brokeneyebooks
instagram.com/brokeneyebooks
patreon.com/brokeneyebooks

BROKEN
eye
BOOKS